# EARTHBOUND

# EARTHBOUND

## JOE HALDEMAN

ACE BOOKS, NEW YORK

**THE BERKLEY PUBLISHING GROUP**
**Published by the Penguin Group**
**Penguin Group (USA) Inc.**
**375 Hudson Street, New York, New York 10014, USA**
Penguin Group (Canada), 90 Eglinton Avenue East, Suite 700, Toronto, Ontario M4P 2Y3, Canada
(a division of Pearson Penguin Canada Inc.)
Penguin Books Ltd., 80 Strand, London WC2R 0RL, England
Penguin Group Ireland, 25 St. Stephen's Green, Dublin 2, Ireland (a division of Penguin Books Ltd.)
Penguin Group (Australia), 250 Camberwell Road, Camberwell, Victoria 3124, Australia
(a division of Pearson Australia Group Pty. Ltd.)
Penguin Books India Pvt. Ltd., 11 Community Centre, Panchsheel Park, New Delhi—110 017, India
Penguin Group (NZ), 67 Apollo Drive, Rosedale, Auckland 0632, New Zealand
(a division of Pearson New Zealand Ltd.)
Penguin Books (South Africa) (Pty.) Ltd., 24 Sturdee Avenue, Rosebank, Johannesburg 2196,
South Africa

Penguin Books Ltd., Registered Offices: 80 Strand, London WC2R 0RL, England

This is an original publication of The Berkley Publishing Group.

FIRST EDITION: December 2011

Library of Congress Cataloging-in-Publication Data

Haldeman, Joe W.
    Earthbound / Joe Haldeman.—1st ed.
        p. cm.
    ISBN 978-0-441-02095-9
    I. Title.
    PS3558.A353E27 2011
    813'.54—dc23            2011035693

PRINTED IN THE UNITED STATES OF AMERICA

10  9  8  7  6  5  4  3  2

*For Gay and Judith, only bound by gravity*

# EARTHBOUND

# 1

I'd been off Earth for so long I didn't recognize the sound of gunfire.

We were walking up a gravel road from the beach at Armstrong Space Force Base, where we'd just watched, I don't know, the end of the world? People were checking phones, watches—nothing electronic was working. Even my wrist tattoo was stuck at 10:23. That's when the rocket we were watching lift off sputtered out and fell into the Pacific.

It didn't explode or anything. It just stopped. Like everything else.

Guns did seem to work, hence the merry popcorn-popping sound. "Get down, Carmen," Namir said conversationally. "We don't know who they're shooting at." Everybody was kneeling or lying on the road, below the level of the sand dunes on both sides. I joined them.

An older man in a white suit, clutching a sun hat to his head, fancy camera on a strap bumping against his chest, came running down the gravel, looking anxiously back at the gunfire.

"Card?" I wouldn't have recognized my brother if he hadn't called a couple of days earlier. He almost slipped on the gravel, but came to rest crouching next to me.

"Sister, love . . ." he was still looking back at the gunfire— "What the fuck is going on? Weren't you supposed to be taking care of all this alien crap?"

"Didn't quite work out," I said. "It's a long story. If we're alive tomorrow, I'll give you chapter and verse."

There were a couple of especially loud bangs, I guessed from bombs or grenades. "Where did Namir go?"

"Back there," his wife Elza said, jerking her thumb toward her other husband, Dustin, who pointed toward Snowbird, who pointed all four arms to the right.

I should note that we were a mixed group, not to say a menagerie: three humans from Earth, three from Mars, and one actual Martian. And now my brother, who was something in between.

Card waved at the Martian Snowbird and tried to croak "hello." He'd stayed on Mars for the required five years, and then escaped back to Earth. Never could speak Martian well, as if anyone could.

"Hello, Card. I remember you much younger."

"Fucking relativity," he said. To me: "You used to be my older sister."

"I guess we'll sort it out somehow." I was born eighty-four years ago, but figured I'd only lived thirty-seven of them. My bratty little brother was twice my age now, in a real sense. From acne to pattern baldness in one stroke.

Namir came clattering back with two automatic weapons under one arm and a holstered pistol in the other hand. He gave the pistol to Elza and a machine gun to Dustin.

That's good. All the spies had guns.

Elza did something complicated with the pistol, inspecting it. "Tell me you found a gun shop behind some dune."

"Didn't kill anybody."

"But somebody's going to be looking for them," Dustin said.

"Not for a while." He looked at Card. "You must be Carmen's brother."

Card nodded. "You must be one of the spies."

"Namir. We have to find someplace less exposed."

"The last place we drove by, did it look like a motor pool?" Elza said.

"I remember, yes. Sandbag wall around it."

"So maybe there's no one there now. Since no vehicles seem to be working."

"We can't just walk up with guns," I said.

"Right. So you go first."

"Once the shooting stops." Actually, I hadn't heard any for a minute or so. "What direction was it coming from?" I asked Card.

"I guess the press and VIP area. They had bleachers set up. They were gonna leave me there even though I had a pass. I paid a guy to take me to the last checkpoint, a half mile from here."

"Glad you found us," I said, and stood up cautiously. The motor pool was about a block away. One low building and dozens of blue NASA trucks and carts. No people obvious. "Paul, let's go."

He got up, and Meryl followed him, and then my brother. "I can talk to the natives," he said. "Lived in California thirty-five years."

"Leave the armed guard with Snowbird," Paul said. "Martians might not be too popular right now."

"Don't risk anybody's life for me," the Martian said. "I won't live long in any case."

"You don't know that," I said lamely.

"I can't live on human food, and only have a few days' worth of mine here. The only renewable source is in the Martian colony in Siberia. I can't walk there—or I could, if I had time, and it might be pleasantly cold. But it would take a long time. I can't live off the land."

"The power could come back any time," Namir said. "We still know nothing about how the Others' minds work."

"No need to comfort me, friend. I lived long enough to swim in the sea."

Namir stared at her for a moment, nodding, and then looked toward me. "Okay, Carmen, go up to the motor pool and nose around. If the coast is clear, give us a signal." He considered that and shook his head, smiling. "I mean, *you* stay here with the gun, and I'll—"

"Don't be such a *man*," Elza said. "Carmen, do you know how to shoot?"

"Never learned, no."

"So you guys go up unarmed and knock on the door. None of that shooting's anywhere near us."

"Okay." Three unarmed space travelers versus God knows how many auto mechanics with wrenches and battery testers.

"Don't try anything aggressive," Namir said. "Just give us the signal, and we'll come up behind the sandbags."

"Or I could scream my lungs out," I said. "Just kidding."

We walked up the incline and then down the paved road. The last of the morning cool had baked off, and the motor pool shimmered in the heat.

"What is it about the power?" Card asked. "I saw the rocket sputter out and crash. But what does that have to do with cars?"

He might be the only person in America who didn't know. Walking down this road, toward us, he couldn't have been watching the cube when it happened.

"The Others pulled the plug," Paul said. "When they disintegrated the moon and filled nearby space with gravel, that was supposed to turn Earth into a 'no space flight' zone." Only last week.

"That seemed pretty obvious. But the rocket jocks had to try anyhow." With heavy shielding and lasers to blast their way through the gravel.

"So they turned off all the free power?" Card said. "That's serious. How long has it been since there were any actual power-generating plants?"

"It's even more serious than that," I said. "Your watch and your cell won't work. It affects batteries; anything electrical."

"Not everything," Meryl said. "Our brains are electromagnetic, electrochemical."

"Smokeless powder works in guns," Paul said, "So I guess chemical energy is okay if it's not making electricity."

"They didn't explain anything," I said. "Just that the free energy we've been using came at the expense of some donor world. As punishment for defying them, we're the donors now."

"For how long?"

"Forever would be a good guess," Paul said. "We've got a lot of adjusting to do."

Card stopped walking and slapped his palm to his forehead. "Jesus. How many people died in the first few seconds?"

"Anyone with artificial organs," Meryl said, "or on life support. Hell, just pacemakers. Tens of millions. Maybe hundreds?"

"People flying," Paul said. "Unless the planes had pilots, and the pilots were able to glide in and land. Not many can do that, without computers. Even if they were near a runway."

Card nodded. "A lot of people in cars. The LA freeways would be a moving junk pile. Everybody on autopilot, going 150."

"Don't cars have failsafes?" I said.

"Yeah, but they're like the opposite of an electromagnet, engine braking. I don't see how they could work without current flowing." My kid brother was suddenly an engineer with a lifetime of experience.

We got to the door of the motor pool building. Paul knocked twice and pushed it open. "Hello? Anybody here?"

"We're over here," a voice reverberated in the gloom. "Who are you?"

"Space Force pilot," he sort of lied. "We were down on the beach, watching the launch."

"So were we." Sound of footsteps coming our way. A man and a woman in blue NASA coveralls came out of the murk. "When we couldn't raise anyone, we came back here. What was that gun-fire?"

"We don't know," Paul said. "Came from the reviewing stand, sounds like."

"Press Relations getting rid of witnesses," the man said.

"Be serious, Wilbur. I'm Katie, this is Wilbur . . ." She pointed at Paul. "You're the famous guy. And you're the Mars Girl."

"When I was a girl." I introduced Meryl.

"You went off to the aliens, the Others." She shook her head. "My grandmother was a girl then, she watched the take-off. Bright-est star in the sky. But you're not, she's eighty-some . . . I guess that relativity does work."

I had to smile. "Seems to work for me."

The man cleared his throat. "The Others are behind this? The rocket failing and the power going off?"

"As punishment," Paul said, and explained what we'd seen. Not everybody had been glued to the cube during the launch. How long would it take for the word to get around? Word of mouth and writ-ten message, carried by hand.

Two more bursts of automatic-weapons fire. Wilbur went to the door and peered out in that direction. "Hope that's our guys."

"Has to be, doesn't it?" Katie said. "But who are they shoot-ing at?"

"Probably just shooting in the air, crowd control. But I wish we had a weapon here, just in case."

"We have a couple," I said, and he looked at me sharply. "We didn't want to look dangerous, walking up here. They're back on the road to the beach, with the rest of us."

"Better bring 'em up."

I started to reach for my cell; how long would that reflex survive? Went to the door and waved both arms.

The four of them came out. "Holy shit!" he said. "Is that a Martian?"

No, it's two ostriches sharing a potato costume. Elza and Dustin trotted toward us; Namir came slowly, covering Snowbird. She was wearing a dirty white smock the size of a tablecloth, dragging along on four legs made for Martian gravity. She liked humans and Earth as abstractions, but I think the reality was getting a little hard on her.

"We heard there was a Martian on the base," Katie said.

"They're not dangerous," Wilbur said.

"Heavens, no." Snowbird might hurt you if she fell on you.

"The three people look dangerous," she said, "though it might be the guns."

"Soldiers," I said, simplifying. "They were with us on the starship." I introduced Elza and Dustin as they sidled in, and then Snowbird and Namir.

"Keep a lookout, Dustin," Namir said. "Thank you for sheltering us. We shouldn't be here long." He gestured toward a long lunch table. "Let's sit."

Namir sat at the head of the table and began disassembling and inspecting his weapon. "If this were a military operation—"

"Which it's not," Paul said quietly.

"We won't forget that. But if it were, there's a standard hierarchy of concern: first ammunition, then water, then food. Communication is in there, irrelevant now, and mobility, which seems to be shoe leather. First ammunition. You don't have any here?"

"No guns," Wilbur said. "Couple of signal-flare pistols in the locker with the life rafts."

"Water, we have plenty of," Katie said, "our own water tank. Not much in the way of food. A snack machine, some left-over bagels."

"Food is going to be the long-term concern, with supply lines broken down. Dustin, tell them about the farm. Fruit Farm?" Namir slapped his gun back together and traded places with Dustin.

"Yeah, the family farm, the commune where I grew up. It's only about a couple of hundred miles to the north."

"I thought they disowned you," I said.

"Well, they did. But that was like seventy years ago. The conservative bunch who ran things will all have died out by now."

"Long walk," Paul said.

"Moving at night," Namir said. "Still, less than ten days."

"How far would you have to walk before you get out of the desert?" I asked.

"Twelve miles," Wilbur said. "Actually, 11.6, going straight west on the access road just north of here. Where is this farm?"

"Near Viva Lento," Dustin said. "Up by the Oregon border."

"Head north on 17," Katie said.

"Good as any. No traffic."

"What are you two going to do?" I asked. "Strength in numbers, if you want to come with us."

"No, I'd better head home," she said.

Wilbur nodded. "No disrespect, Ms. Snowbird, but I don't think I want to be traveling with a Martian."

"I wouldn't either," Snowbird said. You could never tell when they were being ironic, or just logical.

"All of us ought to ransack this place for provisions," Namir said. "Could you show me those snack machines?"

We followed Wilbur through the gloom to the snack bar alcove. There were two machines full of snacks, behind glass, which turned out to be unbreakable plastic. We toppled them over with a crash, and Wilbur found a crowbar that allowed us to break the locks and pry the backs open. Satisfying in an obscure way.

The machines weren't operated by money, but by ration card. So Wilbur or Katie could sit there and get a candy bar every four hours. We didn't have cards, not having yet joined the 22nd century.

While the men ransacked the machines, I went with Katie on a fruitless search for something like knapsacks to carry the booty in. In the mail room, I found a metal cart, a frame that held an empty mail bag and rolled on four sturdy casters. We took it to the water rescue lockers, where I liberated two flare pistols with two belts of four flare rockets each.

Back at the snack bar alcove, we let Katie and Wilbur stuff their pockets and two bags, then arranged the rest into piles according to shelf life, so we could put the relatively perishable things on top. Fruit and sandwiches that had been refrigerated. A drink machine yielded ten liter bottles of water and a couple dozen less useful soft drinks and near beer.

My rolling cart would hold about a quarter of the bounty. Nobody turned up anything like knapsacks, but a storage room had a drawer full of random sizes of cloth bags. Together we could carry all of the water and most of the food. We could leave behind most of the soft drinks and near beer.

Snowbird insisted on carrying two light bags of snacks, though she couldn't eat any of it. She refused water. "I can live a week or more without it. I come from a dry planet." And she wasn't going to last a week unless they turned the power back on.

Katie and Wilbur wished us luck and headed home, facing hours of walking. Neither had family to worry about, but Katie had cats and fish to feed.

"Might as well feed the fish to the cats," Meryl said after they left. "Or fry them up."

Namir was watching them go. "Seem to be nice people. But you never know. They might be back, with others."

"Maybe we should start moving," Dustin said.

"We don't want to travel in daylight. Especially not loaded down with food and water. There will be plenty of people out there with neither, but with guns."

"So let's get some rest while we can," Elza said. "Those of us with weapons stand guard, what, two hours at a time?" We made sure all the doors were locked. The windows were silvered for insulation, so nobody could see us if it was dark inside.

I found a cot in a back room but couldn't sleep, my mind spinning. What if we made the two-week-long trek without incident, and Dustin's family welcomed us into the fold? What about the other seven billion people in the equation?

There wouldn't be seven billion after two weeks. Maybe not half that. I could hardly imagine what the crowded cities would be like.

Even if the governments tried to provide food, water, and shelter for everyone, how could they do it without communication and transportation?

When I was in school, we were told that the world had only three or four months' worth of food in reserve. I suppose that in America most of that was in grain silos, thousands of miles from the population centers on the coasts.

In an abstract sense, I supposed the very poor had the best chance of survival, used to living close to the bottom of the food chain. As if the rich would politely stay away, when the shelves were bare.

I wondered whether Dustin's family had guns. If they were pacifist vegetarians, we might only find their bones.

I must have fallen asleep, because the next thing I knew, Meryl was shaking my shoulder, whispering, "We've got company."

Namir and Elza and Dustin had their guns at the ready. Through the window you could see a ragtag crowd, maybe twenty, and someone was pounding on the door with something heavy and metallic.

None of the people in the crowd had guns visible, but we couldn't see the ones who were pounding on the door.

No police or military uniforms. Most of them wore white nametags.

"I think they're newsies," Card whispered. "And VIPs, from those bleachers where they put me first."

After a minute, most of them moved on, by ones and twos. The one guy kept pounding on the door, rattling the lock. Then he left, too, carrying a metal pipe.

Paul returned from watching out the back windows. "Couple of guys tried to start vehicles. They're gone now."

"How could they start them without keys?"

"Like metal keys?" Card said. "They just have a code you punch into the dash. Those are all N-A-S-A, Wilbur told me."

"What's the firearms law like now, Card?" Namir asked. "Do people have guns at home?"

"California, you can have guns but you can't carry one without a permit, and permits aren't easy to get. That's academic now, I guess."

"Maybe. We'll see how it shakes down. I wonder whether cops will report for duty, and try to enforce the law."

"Where we're headed," Dustin said, "I don't think there'll be much law. Maybe in small towns and some big cities, where cops can work on foot."

"Some people have really big gun collections," Card said. "Dozens of working weapons. Most of them are electric pellet guns, though. Gunpowder and smokeless weapons are expensive, and ammunition is taxed like a hundred bucks a round. Plenty of military and police ammo around now, I guess."

Namir looked at his clip. "I've got a double magazine, forty rounds, and Dustin, you've got a single one?" He nodded.

Elza held up the pistol. "Nine here."

"So we're not getting into any gunfights. We have to assume that any group we encounter with weapons will have more ammunition."

"It's not a war," I said. "We shouldn't even be thinking in those terms. It's more like a natural disaster."

"Unnatural," Dustin said. "I wouldn't wait around for the Red Cross to show up."

"I have a radical thought," Meryl said. "Instead of heading for the hills with guns, why don't we try to *find* something like the Red Cross, and volunteer. Try to do something constructive." That was so like Meryl, social worker to the core.

"It's a good thought," Paul said. "But where would you go; what would you do?"

"It would have to be a city of some size," I said. "Where they might already have charitable organizations in place, with a substantial number of volunteers. With resources for emergency work."

"Like a computer network and ambulances. Helicopters." Namir shook his head. "More useful, they might have first-aid kits. I wouldn't like to be the guy in charge of guarding them, though."

"You think too much like a soldier." Meryl sat down at the table across from him. "That may save our lives some day. But it's not everything. If there's going to be an alternative to chaos, to anarchy, we have to pursue it right away."

"You do that. I'll keep you covered, from behind something solid."

"It's not always about guns!"

"May I say something." Snowbird had all four arms folded, a posture communicating thoughtfulness. "I do not have a dog in this fight, as I once heard a person say. My destiny will not be affected by your decision.

"Namir, your supply of ammunition is small. You have four seconds' worth, and Dustin has two. When it's gone, your weapons are dead weight."

"You can shoot single-shot. And we can find ammunition."

"But there will be people guarding it, who will kill to keep you from it. And how much can you carry? They won't be making any more of it."

"There's probably a lot of it around. But I concede your point."

"If you plan to survive more than weeks or months, violence is the wrong direction. When you run out of ammunition, what will you do?"

Elza did not surprise me: "My husband unarmed is more dangerous than any two men with guns."

"A nice sentiment," he said, "but I want to choose the two men.

"But Snowbird is right, in the long run. Card, walking north, what would be the nearest city?"

"Depends on what you would call a city. Custer City, technically. But don't try to get a good meal there."

"How far?"

"Twenty-five miles, I guess."

"That's about as far as we're going to get on this amount of water."

Card smiled. "Have you tried a tap?"

"What?"

"This isn't a spaceship. You turn on a faucet anywhere, and water comes out."

That caught me, too. Live on recycled pee for years, and you start to feel real personal about water.

A shed outside had armloads of empty plastic gallon jugs. We didn't take the ones that smelled of solvent, and rinsed the others well—just by turning a tap and letting gravity do the work. How long that would last, of course, we had no way of telling. You could see the water tank a couple of blocks away. One stray bullet could empty it. Or an aimed one.

The sun would be up for a few more hours. Paul and Namir took binoculars up on the roof and didn't see any gatherings of people: just a few individuals and pairs. Paul came down with a suggestion.

"We ought to go find out whether our celebrity is worth anything. Go back to that headquarters building and find out what's happening, anyhow." A reasonable suggestion that made my knees weak.

"I'll come along as a guard," Namir said.

"No; no guns. We'll probably be safer without." He looked at Meryl, who smiled and nodded.

I wasn't so sure. We didn't have a magic wand that would make other people's guns disappear.

Elza held out her pistol, handle first. "Paul, at least take this. You must have had some training in the Space Force."

He took it and stared at it. "One afternoon, back in '62. This is the safety?" She nodded, and he put the pistol in his waistband, out of sight under his shirt. "Thanks. Pray we don't need it."

I put two bottles of water and some snacks in a bag, and slung it over my shoulder. I'd lost my sun hat down on the beach, so pulled a faded NASA cap off a peg. Paul straightened it. "Now we're official."

"If you're not back in two hours, we'll come after you," Namir said. I checked my wrist tat and it was still 10:23, for the rest of my life.

"Make it three," Paul said, without suggesting how either of them could tell time—some secret military thing, no doubt. "Take us half an hour just to walk there."

"Careful by the bleachers," Card said, unnecessarily. Paul nodded and went out the door.

It was a relief to be alone with him, the first time since we'd left the billet at dawn. He took my hand and squeezed it. "You and me."

"Me and you," I said automatically. A song refrain from when I was eighteen. Paul an ancient man of twenty-nine.

We walked in silence for a minute. "It's a lot to take in."

"I'm still trying to sort it out."

"Guess we're all still in shock." He laughed. "Except Snowbird. The only one who knows for sure she's going to die."

"Poor thing."

"Poor us. Poor whole fucking human race. How many will be alive a year from now? A month from now?"

"In a month, they'll still be eating groceries," I said.

He nodded. "In a year, each other."

"Save you for last." I pinched his butt. "You always were a tough old bastard."

We both laughed. Keeping that one monster at bay.

There was a lot of trash on the road, with no wind to blow it around. Press releases and promotion packets, as well as cups and food trash. And this wasn't the main avenue out; people who lived in California would be going the other way. Assuming they were headed home.

A couple of hundred yards before we got to the bleachers, there were the first signs of violence. Dark spatters of blood, dried in the dust.

No bodies at first, but then Paul followed a trail of drops to a place behind a portable toilet. A woman in sexy silver shorts, who had been wounded in the abdomen. She'd held it in with her hands for a couple of dozen steps, and then collapsed. Her guts were a pile of glistening gray and blue, awash in blood. Paul checked her pulse while I usefully leaned the other way and vomited. He held my shoulders while I gagged and coughed the last of it, and handed me a water bottle.

"We don't have to go any farther," he said.

"We do," I said, my voice a hoarse croak.

"It will probably get worse." He started to pull out the pistol, and I leaned against him.

"Leave it hidden. Someone might be watching."

"Of course." He put his arm around me, and we continued up the road toward the HQ building.

"Look at the brass. Someone stood here and fired toward the bleachers." A scatter of brass shell casings to our left.

"Or up in the air," I said. "No more bodies."

"That's something." He stopped. "This isn't smart. Let's go back to—"

We were maybe twenty yards from the entrance to the temporary building. A tall fat man stepped out onto the wooden deck, brandishing a weapon, and fired a burst into the air. "Y'all put up your hands?"

We did. He clumped down the three steps to the ground. "Look what we got, Jemmie. Y'all from that spaceship. The starship. Saw you on the cube last night."

"We are," Paul said.

Another person, presumably Jemmie, stepped out of the darkness. He was also holding a weapon, and binoculars with a strap dangling. "Been watchin' you. You come up from the motor pool."

They were both wearing NASA coveralls, spotless, with the fold lines still visible. Jemmie's were a couple of sizes too large, the sleeves rolled up.

"You work for NASA?" I said.

"Guess we do now," the fat one said. "You wanta help me launch my rocket?"

Paul tensed. *Don't!* "We don't mean you any harm," I said.

"I bet you don't." The fat one stepped forward, his weapon on Paul, looking at me.

"You keep it in your pants, Howard. Bet they got that god-damn Martian back there." He stepped down to join us. "Don't you."

"I don't know who's down there now," Paul improvised. "You saw a Martian in the binoculars?"

"He was with you all on the cube this morning, before it got shut off."

"And the other aliens did that," Howard said.

"Time we did something back," Jemmie said, pointing his weapon down the road. "Let's us go have a talk with Mr. Martian." He started walking. "Then we figure out what to do with you all."

Howard came alongside me and put his big arm on my shoulder.

"They say you was with all those men fifty years." He grabbed my breast, hard. "Don't seem possible—"

I was going to give him an elbow to the ribs, hesitated, and heard a tiny metallic click. Then there was a huge explosion and a shower of blood and gore in front of me.

Then some voices I could hardly hear, my ears ringing. At first I thought all the blood was mine; I was dead. But then Howard fell in front of me, hard, the top of his skull shattered, an artery still pulsing.

I turned around and saw the other man, Jemmie, trying to run backwards, both his hands out to protect himself from Paul's pistol. Paul had the pistol gripped in both hands, but they were shaking so violently he probably couldn't have hit the man if they were in a small room together.

I saw all this in a strange state of floating calm, realizing that the little sound I'd heard before I went deaf had been the safety on his pistol.

The man was running like a sprinter now. Paul fired once over the man's head, and stooped to pick up the weapon he'd dropped or thrown down.

I looked back at the big man dying, his arms and legs moving feebly as the blood spurt slowed to a drizzle. He'd shit his new blue trousers. I leaned over and burped a little acid, and opening my mouth wide made my ears crackle, and some hearing came back.

Paul came up from behind and gathered me to him, still shaking hard, sharp sweat smell and gunsmoke. "Killed him. Jesus fucking Christ."

I was still floating, stunned. "That's the most religious thing you've ever said to me."

❄

**From *Rear View Mirror: an Immediate History*, by Lanny del Piche (Eugene, 2140):**

. . . there is no way to calculate how many people died in the first second, minute, or hour. A week later, when there was still food, perhaps one billion of the globe's seven billion had perished. Failure of transportation systems and medical life support—which almost claimed this writer's life—accounted for a large fraction of those deaths immediately. Most died in violence, though, after the total collapse of civil and military authority. As far as I know, no truly large city, more than ten million people, survived the initial crisis well, except perhaps for the religious police states in the Middle East and America's new Confederacy. (But I don't think either would last very long without supporting technology to keep the desert at bay; without wealth to trade for water.)

Civilization, in the broad social sense of the word, obviously has survived in smaller towns and cities around the world. This writer met a couple who had sailed from Australia to California, who said that life was reasonably comfortable and secure in a string of hundreds of fishing villages spread along Australia's eastern and southeastern coasts, and in the Great Barrier Reef. Here in Oregon, we have had sailing visitors from as far south as Costa Rica, and as far north as the Aleutian Islands. No sailors have come from Europe, Africa, or the American east coast, which leads us to believe that the Panama Canal is not open.

A few individuals and small parties have made it here from the East Coast and Midwest by horseback or bicycle. I've heard of people who walked all the way, but haven't met any, and would not be inclined to believe them. That would be a long walk in less than two years.

The tales these travelers bring are not usually happy. Most of the heavily populated parts of the East are burial grounds, or just boneyards. There are towns like this one, able to guard enough land to grow subsistence crops, and keep a moderately large population safe from marauders.

Of course these towns tend to be on rivers or lakes, in temperate or warmer climes. The surviving population of Florida is probably ten times that of New England.

(The people who originally settled this country from Europe did live in the north, and had to deal with killing winters. They wouldn't have done so well, though, surrounded by millions of starving people with guns. Hard to get a farm going when people will kill for one ear of corn.)

Fortunately, ammunition is getting scarce . . .

# 2

I felt Paul wave and turned around to see Namir running toward us, his rifle pointed down at a slant. "We're okay," he said, too softly for Namir to hear.

Still holding me, he turned partway around, to look in the direction the man had been running. "I think he went back into the HQ building. Here." He handed me the pistol. "Sit down behind me."

He sat down cross-legged and planted his elbows on his knees, bringing the man's rifle up to sight down the barrel. He clicked a switch, I guess a safety, several times.

The pistol was heavier than it looked. The barrel was warm. I kept my finger away from the trigger.

Namir ran up and hesitated, looking at the body, and then got down prone next to us and pointed his rifle in the same direction. "Somebody in there?"

"I think so. I've got his weapon."

"Probably more in there. Come on!" He sprang across the road to where a panel truck was stalled sideways. "Get cover." We followed him and crouched down behind it.

"So what happened?"

"Two guys wanted to go down to the motor pool and kill a Martian. They didn't know we had Elza's pistol."

"That one grabbed me." I pointed at the body. "Grabbed my breast."

"And you shot him in the head. Remind me to mind my manners."

"I shot him," Paul said. "Had to. It was obvious they . . . they weren't . . ." He swallowed hard.

"Weren't going to let you live," Namir said. "Good you thought fast."

"I didn't think at all." He left the truck's cover and walked over to the man he'd killed. He nudged the man's body with his toe. "Fuck." He kicked him. "Shit. Fuck." Kicked him harder.

I ran over and held him, then pulled him so close I could feel his heart's hammer in my own chest. Felt him kick again and again. "Fucking shit," he sobbed.

My eyes stinging wet on his chest, I echoed him, fucking shit. Strong and meaningless words.

"Get back here," Namir said. "Please! You're sitting ducks." He fired a short burst at the door.

Paul snapped out of it and hurried back, with me staggering in tow. "Sorry," he said to Namir, as we got down next to him. "Never done that before."

Namir squeezed his shoulder and nodded, not taking his eyes off the door.

A spot of white appeared in one corner of the door, a white cloth being waved. "Show yourself," Namir shouted. "Hands up."

He stepped into the light, blinking, still waving the white flag, which turned out to be underwear.

"Don't shoot. I don't have no gun."

"Who else is in there?"

"Ain't nobody now." He started to gesture.

"Keep your hands showing!" To Paul he said quietly, "Stand up with the gun. Aim it at him but stay behind cover." Then he stood and started walking toward the man.

"One move and you're dead. If anyone else shows up, you die first."

He got close enough to point the rifle right between the man's eyes. "Now turn around, slowly." He did.

"We're going into that building. You're certain there's no one in there?"

"Nobody I know of."

"If I see one person, I'll blow your brains out."

"One dead guy! There was one dead guy, maybe two."

"If they're still dead, you're safe." He tapped him on the back of the head with the rifle's muzzle, and the man flinched. "Move it."

"This doesn't look smart," I whispered to Paul. "How does he know he's not walking into an ambush?"

"He's the expert." He thought for a moment. "Maybe he's assuming that if there were someone armed in there, he would have fired at us while we were exposed. But he has to know for sure before we turn our backs on the building."

"Maybe." Or maybe, I thought, Namir was going to kill the man in cold blood, and didn't want to do it in front of us.

They went inside the building, and I waited for the shot.

It didn't come. They shuffled back out, and Namir said something to him, and he ran away at top speed. Namir kept the gun pointed in his direction but walked casually toward us.

"The place is a mess. A man and a woman dead, and it looks like someone sprayed around the whole control room with automatic fire. Nothing there for us."

"What do you think happened?" I asked.

"No idea. That man, Jemmie, said it was like that when they came in. He's probably lying, but I don't think he or the other killed those two. They were shotgunned."

"They might have used a shotgun and then discarded it," Paul said.

Namir nodded and shrugged. " 'Every man shall die for his own sins.' I had to either let him go or kill him."

"We couldn't take him with us," I said, but didn't like the idea of him being out there and brutally angry.

"Let's go back to the motor pool," Namir said. "Wait for darkness."

"Or the U.S. Marines," Paul said, "whichever comes first."

·❊·

Elza was waiting for us at the door. I handed her pistol back. "It works."

"We saw, through the binoculars. Good thing you had it."

"It was." Though I'd been thinking of it more as a curse than a blessing.

"You should go talk to your brother. He's not taking this well."

"The shooting?"

She shook her head. "He didn't see that. Just things in general."

The end of civilization? How childish of him. "Where is he?"

"Snack room."

He was sitting cross-legged under the skylight with six empty near-beer cans in a pyramid in front of him. Pretty fast work. Thirty minutes?

"Card—"

"I saw Paul kill that man."

"Yeah; me too. See?" I turned to show him the speckles and spatters of blood and gore on my left shoulder.

He nodded, looking at it as if it were a shirt pattern. "I couldn't be part of it anymore."

"You're not going through one tenth what Paul is." Not to mention your sister. "He's never killed before."

"I know, I know. But you don't understand."

"I guess I don't."

He took the can off the top of the pyramid and sucked at it. "I have three physical identities. Had. The other two are completely, were completely, electronic. They could take external forms—rent-a-bodies—when it was convenient, but they didn't have to.

"For most of my life, when this original body became uncomfortable, I could step out of it, and automatic repair nanosystems would take over, while I stayed in one of the other two bodies."

"You mean if your *brain* makes you uncomfortable?"

"Brain, endocrine system, gonads. The parts that generate and mediate emotional states."

"Well, welcome to reality."

He had another drink and shook his head, wincing. "Just what I'd expect you to say, Carmen. But there are all kinds of reality. This one is shallow and painful and inescapable."

"But this one is the real world."

"Not to me. Not to billions of perfectly real people."

We had talked about this a little on the cube two days ago. But I guess to me it was just a more vivid and time-consuming version of the VR games that had so dominated his time when he was a kid. To my great annoyance and our parents' exasperation.

"Sorry I'm being such a Sal the Sal," he said, dragging a long-dead pop star from our mutual childhood, an egotistical brat. "It's almost an automatic reflex, switching over, and my body wonders why it's alive and suffering."

"You're *dead* while it happens?"

"Sure, this body. You can't be in two places at once."

Creepy. "Well, I can see that it's a terrible loss. Worse than your best friend dying."

"They were both *me*! Dying. And I think this third me could die if I will it."

"Don't even think of it, Card. You're all the family I have."

"And your only native guide. It's nice to feel wanted."

# 3

Nice to have a native guide, but as darkness fell, I might have traded him for a map and a flashlight. A big box of kitchen matches wouldn't hurt. Did they still have them in this future?

We had lined up all our gear by the door and opened it a crack to watch the light fade. The cloudless sky went from lemon to salmon to deepening gray.

It was no surprise, of course, to see meteors crisscrossing as the sky got darker; we'd been seeing that ever since the Others blew up the moon. Really bright ones rolled across the daytime sky so often that no one commented on them anymore. But there was a new feature that we hadn't noticed while there was still power, and the lights of civilization: night would never be completely dark.

That cloud of debris that was the corpse of the moon was composed of trillions of pebbles and rocks that all reflected sunlight like tiny moons. The result was a dim haze that made enough light to see your hand a few feet away.

Paul was mortified that he hadn't predicted it, with his graduate degree in astrophysics. Of course, we hadn't seen a night sky without city lights since we had landed on Earth four days before.

Our plan to sneak up to the farm under cover of darkness was useless. There would be plenty of people on the road at night, avoiding the desert heat.

Snowbird gave voice to the obvious. "You have to leave me behind. I'm like a beacon, drawing trouble. And I slow you down."

"We're responsible for you," Namir said.

"Not really. I would as soon die here as anywhere, and I would rather not take any of my friends with me.

"Perhaps I will just swim away until I tire out and sink. I would be the best Martian swimmer on Earth. Or anyplace."

"Thank you for the generosity, but we can't abandon you." In the dim murk, I couldn't read the others' expressions. "Are we in agreement here?"

"No," Dustin said. "Snowbird, I also appreciate your logic and selflessness. I really think I would make the same offer if I were in your shoes. In your position. Who is with me?"

There was some muttering and throat clearing, cut short by a loud thump that was the butt of Namir's rifle hitting the floor. "We are not going to cast lots over whether to allow one of our number to die.

"The seven of us are alone here. We traveled fifty light-years together in constant danger and considerable discomfort. We faced a powerful and implacable enemy and survived. We watched our universe change drastically three separate times. Whatever is going to happen to us, we face it together.

"Snowbird, consider extending your logic and generosity. If some idiot kills you for being a Martian, you will be exactly as dead as if you had drowned. Meanwhile, you might be the most valuable member of this ragtag bunch."

"You're our wild card," Paul said. "I think you're the only Martian in the hemisphere. You're closer to understanding the Others than any human can be, and they're still the primary enemy, no matter how far away they are in space and time."

Elza stood up in the darkness. "The enemy I'm worried about now are assholes like the ones you dealt with today. So what are we going to do now? I mean tonight. If we can't benefit from darkness, maybe we should stay here until morning and start moving then, when no one can sneak up on us."

"That's right," Namir said. "Another six or eight hours' rest wouldn't hurt us, either."

"Leaving two of us on guard while the others sleep," Elza said.

"One up on the roof, with the binoculars," Paul said. "That should be me. I can use the stars to measure out two-hour shifts."

"Show us how?" Namir said.

I saw Paul's silhouette as he opened the door to look out. "Sure. It's dark enough." The brighter stars were visible through the sky glow.

We all filed out, including Snowbird—never can tell when reading the stars might come in handy, for a doomed Martian stranded in the Mojave Desert.

It was possible to come close to calculating the actual local time, if you knew the date and a few constellations. But none of us had appointments to meet, so he just showed us an easy way to approximate the passage of time. Your fist at arm's length is about ten degrees. The sun or moon or a star moves about thirty degrees, three fists, in two hours.

(Meryl was able to use her xenology background—she knew better than the rest of us how the world looked to a Martian—and patiently translated what Paul had showed us into Snowbird's anatomy. She did have a lot more fists to work with.)

I drew the first shift, with Paul on the roof, but Namir was out there, too, hidden behind a truck. Not tired enough to sleep, he said.

He had showed us all how to operate the rifles and pistol, and made us practice loading and unloading and safety procedures until we could do the whole drill with our eyes closed.

It didn't make me too confident. The rifle was heavy and cold and greasy, and smelled of gunsmoke. My skin still crawled where the man's blood and brains had spattered me.

I'd vomited twice again, mostly water and acid.

I was hungry but didn't want to waste food by barfing.

So I tried to force myself into calm, but I couldn't not think about the sudden explosion and gory splash.

Namir had asked whether I would like to be excused from the guard schedule because of the traumatic experience. I said no, that feeling as if I could protect myself would help. Maybe it would. Not yet.

I was next to the front door, behind a stack of sandbags scavenged from the wall. I could crouch behind them and shoot over the top of the stack, or lie down—"assume the prone position," which sounds like a porn director's command. Or I could curl up into a ball and weep.

There was a hole in the sky, which was interesting. I actually figured it out for myself before Paul had a chance to enlighten me: it was the Earth's shadow, blocking off sunshine from the lunar debris. Sort of an anti-moon, a little bigger than the moon and moving much faster through the sky.

The constant meteor shower seemed to be slowing down, or maybe I was just getting used to it.

There was a quiet rustle behind me, and I started. But it was only Snowbird.

"I wondered whether you were ready to eat," she said. She held out something that touched my arm.

"Thanks." It was some kind of candy bar. I unwrapped it and was grateful for the creamy chocolate and unidentifiable nuts. "How are you doing?"

"I'm in a complex state, which is also simple. Preparing to die."

"In Mars, I suppose it would be much different." I knew a little about their death customs. "With your family."

She shuffled in the dark. "Newsies called it telepathy, but it's nothing so strange. More like a data transfer. We don't quite understand how it works, but the result is clear. Experiences that are unique to the dying individual are transferred to a sort of family memory. Like adding to a scrapbook in a human family, but all in the head."

"You would have a lot of those. Unique experiences."

She made a two-click sound of agreement. "I don't think anything will be transferred without physical contact, though."

"The more reason for you not to give up."

There was a long pause. "You really think the Others will turn the power back on?"

"Anybody's guess. I don't suppose it's likely. Do you?"

"My instinct says no. They aren't kindly." That was an understatement. "But it's hard to predict where their logic may have taken them."

The Others think very fast, superconducting neurocircuits, but they live and move with glacial slowness, slithering through liquid nitrogen. Their dealings with species like ours are planned out years ahead of time, or even centuries or millennia. Their automata, who perceive and react at our speed or faster, observe us and decide which branch of the logic tree to follow. The decision to turn off the free power doomed a billion or more humans, but as far as we know it was just remorseless logic, a chain of events that started tens of thousands of years ago. If humans do this, then we will do *this*, in self-defense.

Many races on earthlike planets have been evaluated this way. They say that many were not destroyed.

As we weren't, quite. Yet.

"They haven't been unkind to you. To Martians."

"No, but we aren't competitors. It bothers me to think that we're not particularly useful to them anymore. We were created for a purpose and have fulfilled it."

The Others created the Martians, biological machines, and put them in an Earth-like bubble in Mars, to serve as an advance warning, in case the unpleasant denizens of Earth evolved into space flight.

It was illustrative of the Others' slow, tortuous, logical method. When we finally were sophisticated enough to leave Earth, one of our first targets would be Mars. When we found the Martian underground city, that would trigger a signal to Neptune's moon Triton, where an individual Other was resting in frigid nitrogen slush. It would evaluate the situation and choose among various preordained courses of action.

It chose a scenario where humans and Martians had to work together to defuse a bomb that would destroy all advanced life on Earth. Then it went back to its home planet, almost twenty-five light-years away, to report.

One assumes that the Others were ready and waiting, when it came back with news of what it had done and learned. The one best course of action was chosen, and the tools for it sent back almost twenty-five light-years to the waiting Earth.

In the intervening fifty years, though, the Earth had built an interplanetary defense fleet, which was obviously not unexpected.

Those thousand defensive ships posed no real threat to the Others; their home was a million times farther away. But the ships represented a dangerous attitude, as many had feared, and the Others had a plan for that.

The Others didn't destroy us all, though that would've been simple, but just pulverized the moon, scattering its material more or less evenly inside the former satellite's orbit, which destroyed the fleet and sent an unambiguous message: stay on Earth. Our glorious leaders opted to ignore that, or defy it, which triggered another pre-ordained response, taking away not only their gift of free energy, but somehow all electrical power as well. Suddenly marooning us in the nineteenth century, surrounded by useless sophisticated hardware. Like flashlights.

"Someone's coming," Snowbird whispered. I couldn't see anyone.

"Halt!" Paul shouted from the roof. "Put your hands up." The binoculars would help him see.

"I'm not armed," a scared voice said. A young woman or younger boy.

"I see her," Namir said. "Carmen, she's directly in front of you, maybe thirty feet away. Please leave your weapon and go search her. I have you covered."

That does a lot of good, I thought. If something goes wrong, you can shoot in our general direction.

"I'm over here," she said. "Over here, over here, over here. I don't mean anybody any harm." About halfway there, I could see her, a dark ghost in the dim sky light, dressed in black, her hands pale smudges over her head.

"Excuse me," I said idiotically, and patted her the way they did in cop shows fifty and a hundred years ago. She was about my size, but muscular. If she had a weapon on her, it was stuck in a place I was reluctant to touch.

Her clothing was like satin, and it was a strangely strong erotic experience, caressing a person I'd never seen. Maybe with proper study I could become a lesbian.

"Okay. So who are you, and what are you doing here? All dressed in black." Her skin was evidently dark, except for her palms.

"I'm Alba Larimer. Security officer here at Armstrong. I came to warn you—some people plan to ambush you and take the Martian."

"What do they plan to do with her?" Namir asked. He was still behind the truck.

"They think the Other must be watching us, the one that was on the cube?" The one we knew as Spy. "They think if they threaten to kill her, the Other will show up and make a deal."

"That is stupid on so many levels," Namir said. "But thank you. My name is Namir. Do you know where the ambush would be?"

"Somewhere between here and the turnoff to Route 17. Probably a building. There are a couple of dozen, unfortunately. You'd probably be better off staying here, if you have guns. Let them approach a defended position."

She was talking his language.

"Hm. How many of them?"

"Only two were talking. There might have been more outside."

"And what is your stake in this?"

"My *job*," she said, her voice shaking. "No one has relieved me of my responsibilities."

I could almost see him nodding, assessing her. "Security. Do you have access to weapons and ammunition?"

"An assault rifle, a shotgun, and riot gear. In my car's trunk, I'm afraid. Electronic lock."

"We have an electronic crowbar," Paul said from above. "How far away?"

"Less than a half mile; I was watching the launch."

"What do you think?" Paul said.

I was not sure what to say, and then Namir answered. "I'll go with her. Alba, can you find your car in this darkness?"

"Yes; it's white. It's exposed, though, by the side of the road."

"Let's move quickly, then. I'll get the crowbar."

Paul offered to come along as backup, and Namir said no, period. He didn't have to explain. If she turned out to be a bad guy, we were only risking one man and one weapon. And she didn't yet know how few people and weapons we had.

"Is there a central security building," I asked, "where they keep all the guns and all?"

"I walked there first. It was a mess. At least three officers dead inside. I let myself in through the kitchen, and nobody saw me. That's when I overheard the plot to kidnap the Martian."

"So they're armed to the teeth."

"I don't think so. The armory went into automatic lockdown when the power went off. I don't think you can get in there without a heavy-duty laser or a cutting torch."

"The lock would be mechanical," Paul said, "I wonder if there's a mechanical way around it . . . probably not. It wouldn't have been designed with the idea that the power would go off forever."

"Do you think it really is forever? I didn't see the broadcast."

"I don't remember the exact wording," I said. "It sounded pretty final."

"They said we were to become a 'donor planet,' " Paul said. "So some other world would be getting free power at the expense of our own potential for generating electricity. Or that's how I interpret it."

"Are you a scientist?"

"No. Used to be a rocket jock. Currently unemployed."

I could feel her smile. "Aren't we all, now."

I heard a loud clank and muttered curse from inside. Namir had found the crowbar by knocking it over.

He was just visible, coming through the door. Rifle slung over his shoulder, crowbar held like a weapon in his right hand.

"Carmen, you move up to the edge of the wall. Take the safety off. If we draw any fire, shoot high in our direction. We'll run back as fast as we can."

"We'll probably be okay," Alba said. "I haven't seen or heard anyone nearby." She laughed. "Though I didn't see or hear you, Namir, when I walked in."

"Good. I've been trying to stay invisible. Let's go."

I followed them as far as the entrance, then settled in, leaning against the sandbags. Which smelled like the beach, plastic and hot sand.

Alba disappeared immediately into the murk, but I could still see Namir for a minute. Then he was gone.

I was straining to hear, and so jumped at the first loud noise. A good thing I didn't have my finger on the trigger. It was just Namir attacking the car trunk with the crowbar. Then a loud pop, and a vague sound of metal things clicking against metal in the distance. Then several dull thuds, which I supposed were Namir trying to break into an unbreakable window.

This would be the dangerous time. People would be attracted by the noise and follow the sound.

It stopped, and I watched and listened anxiously for several minutes.

Then something moved on the road in front of me. "Namir?" I whispered.

"It's me."

"And Alba." I couldn't see her until they passed directly in front of me. An advantage to being black.

"Paul," Namir stopped, and said to the roof, "is it two hours yet?"

"Just about."

"I'll send Elza up to relieve you." He reached out and touched my arm. "You can get some rest now, Carmen. Give Dustin your rifle and send him back. I'll bring Alba up to speed."

I felt a momentary irrational twinge of jealousy. The black widow comes out of the night and claims our protector. But I really could use some sleep.

# 4

I woke to pale light and quiet conversation. Got up stiffly from the pile of laundered uniforms I'd used as bedding. Rubbed my face and dragged fingers through my hair and realized I would kill for a toothbrush. Found the rear sink and rinsed my mouth and splashed my face, and went toward the sound.

Alba was talking to Paul. Please let her be ugly.

Of course she was not. Regular features, intelligence in her eyes. A nice figure that I'd gotten to paw before Paul could even fantasize about it.

"You must be Carmen."

"I don't know. It's early yet." I took her hand. Able was I ere I saw Alba. "This is the stuff from your car?"

"Combined with your pistol, yes. Wish we had more ammunition. At least all the rifles use the same kind." Two pistols and a new-looking rifle—our two must have been in use—and a mean-looking thing that I guessed was the "riot gun." I picked it up carefully.

"Ten gauge," she said. "It makes a hell of a noise, but we only have one box of shells for it. Can't get them at Kmart."

"Must kick like a mule."

"No, it's recoilless. The rounds are like little rockets. And nobody but me can fire it; it's keyed to my thumbprint."

"What will they think of next?"

"I'd like to ask Alba to join us," Paul said. "She brings expertise and local knowledge as well as weapons."

We looked at each other, and a certain understanding passed. She wasn't a danger where Paul was concerned, at least not yet. "And a knapsack," I said, looking down at the gear. "Tear gas grenades, two canteens. What are these?" I gingerly touched one of four things that looked like rubber balls painted green.

"Flash-bangs. You can temporarily blind and deafen an adversary without hurting him." She pointed at one. "You click the red dot twice and throw; it'll go off when it hits the ground."

"Do they come with earplugs and dark glasses?"

She laughed. "Long gone. We have to improvise."

There were four boxes of rifle ammunition, smaller than the box for the riot gun. Nothing that I could see for the pistol. "We're not exactly ready for a war, are we?"

"In more ways than one, no." She glanced at Paul. "Paul told me what happened to you both yesterday. I've never gone through anything like that. I mean, I trained for the eventuality, and thought it through, but I've never shot anybody or been shot at."

"Does the prospect bother you?"

"It makes me sick. Ten percent excited and ninety percent sick."

"Here comes the expert," Paul said. Namir came in shirtless, rubbing his face with a towel. His muscles weren't as well defined as they had been on the starship. No real exercise for a week.

"There's a story that's reinvented every war," he said, "that goes back at least to the nineteenth century . . . someone asks a sniper what he feels when he takes aim and squeezes, and a man falls dead. He says 'Recoil.'"

"I did that when I was a boy, eighteen or nineteen. We had smart bullets; you kept them on target with a joystick. And there *was* a kind of joy when you hit the target, hand-slapping and thumbs-up—it was a group effort, and the guy you killed was just a grainy black-and-white image, like a pocket video game.

"But I've done the opposite extreme, too. After Gehenna, I killed a man with my bare hands. Tried to strangle him, but he resisted hard. Finally beat his head against the concrete floor until . . . until he died. I felt a different kind of joy then, fierce. But horror, too, like I could never get my hands clean again."

"Gehenna," she said quietly. "We studied it."

"The bastards killed my mother. And almost everyone I worked with, in Mossad. Tel Aviv, what, seventy years ago?"

"Seventy-one," she said, good student.

"And you've been shot, too," I said.

He nodded. "New York City. I stepped off a slidewalk and a woman was waiting for me. One shot, point-blank in the chest."

"Killed you?"

"Yeah, but I was back in a couple of minutes. A pro would've gone for the head."

"Was she a spy like you?"

"Just a hire, we think. My bodyguard did go for the head—'two in the chest, one in the head,' as we were taught. So we couldn't find out from her who she was, who she worked for. He got hell for that, demoted. Unfair."

He picked up the new rifle and removed the magazine and the bolt, the way he'd showed us, and inspected the bolt minutely. "I'd thought that part of my life was long over." He slid the top two rounds out of the magazine and put them back, testing the spring with his thumb, and then removed the top round again and set it on the table. "Better to have one less round than jam. Spring is old."

He looked up. "Your name is Alba?"

"That's right."

"Scotland?"

"No, it means 'dawn' in Spanish."

"Your father was . . ."

"Five cc's of thawed-out Harvard sperm. Never met the guy."

He nodded, looking off in the distance. "That must feel strange. Your father might have been dead when you were conceived."

"I've thought about that myself. I was never curious enough to check."

"Understandable." He looked around. "Did we all lose fathers and mothers on this trip?"

Fifty years evaporated by relativity. "Meryl talked to her parents," I said, "both of them. Don't know whether they'd survive the power going off."

He looked at the cartridge in his hand. "These aren't smart rounds. Tracers?"

"Every fourth."

"Mixed blessing." I supposed because they made a line that pointed back to your own position.

"Are we going to stay here or leave?" I said.

"They know we're here?" Namir asked Alba.

"Motor pool, yes."

"I think we should wait for them. They'll get impatient, today or tomorrow. How many?"

"Three I know of. The ones I overheard at HQ."

Namir stood and stretched. "If I were them, I'd find sniper positions, separate ones, and wait. Pick us off one at a time. Who's on the roof?"

"Dustin," Paul said.

"I'll go up and make sure he's keeping his head down. Roof's the obvious first target for a sniper." He checked his wrist for the non-existent watch, made a face, and went toward the stairs.

"Is he hard to live with?" Alba asked, after Namir had left.

"No. He's very considerate and calm."

"Controlled," Paul said. "He's been through enough to send anybody right 'round the bend. That one he talked about wasn't the only person he's killed." He shook his head hard. "God. Now I'm one, too, a killer."

"You had to do it, Paul."

"So did he. So did he."

"He's stable, though," Alba said. "Seems about as solid as anyone I've ever met."

Paul laughed. "That's what they always say in the newsie interviews. 'Who would ever have thought a man that *stable* would kill his mother and eat her?' But yeah. We lived together for years in that crowded starship, and I never saw him lose his temper."

"Which is unnatural," I had to point out. "The rest of us had our little moments."

"Like Moonboy. A little assault and battery."

"I heard about him, on the cube show about you. He went crazy, and the Others killed him?"

"Not really," I said. "They took him, but he's not dead, if they're to be believed."

"Not alive, either. A kind of suspended animation, which he'll never leave. Close enough to being dead."

Something I hadn't thought of in a while. "Alive or dead or in between, he's the only human they have in their possession, to study. The only one of us who cracked under the strain."

"Of course they knew that," Paul said. "And we were all glad. He was a real pain in the butt, as well as a lunatic."

"Talking about my Moonboy?" Meryl said as she walked into the room, brushing her hair.

"Sorry," we both said.

"Don't be. He *was* a lunatic and a pain in the ass. Ask Elza." He'd been in bed with Elza when he had his breakdown, and punched her hard enough to break her nose. Meryl was not surprised by the infidelity then, but she had been by the violence.

"We were all supposedly chosen because we could get along with others in close quarters," I said.

"Some things you just can't test for." There was real pain behind her brusqueness. "So are we moving out now?" We told her about the new plan, or non-plan. She went into the kitchen to hard-boil all the eggs, for portability.

Namir came down and went around checking doors and windows. He came back with Snowbird. "Snowbird, this is Alba."

She made a little curtsy, like a horse in dressage. "You are black."

"Yeah, and you smell funny."

"I apologize for catabolism. I have no food to metabolize." In fact, she was starting to smell like marigolds. "I've not seen a black person since I left Mars, many years ago."

"You've been stuck here since you got back?"

"Here on the base, yes, in protective custody."

"Serious threats on her life," I said. "Even before the shit hit the fan."

"The *what*?"

"Old expression. One of my father's favorites."

"How much longer can you live," Namir asked, "without new food?"

"I have no idea. I've never been hungry before."

"You can't eat any human food?" Alba asked.

"No. I can consume pure carbohydrates but get no nutrition from them. And the smallest amount of protein contamination would kill me."

"They didn't have food for you anywhere on this base?" I said.

"A few days' worth, which I've eaten. More was coming, from Russia. Actually, if the power hadn't gone out, I might have joined the other Martians there by now, or at least tomorrow—"

There was a sudden gunshot. Namir snatched the rifle off the table and hit the floor, hard. *"Get away from the window!"* Snowbird half galloped into the next room. I slumped myself down behind the table. They couldn't see in, I thought irrelevantly. They could *shoot* in.

Elza came staggering into the room, rubbing sleep from her eyes. "What was—"

Paul grabbed her, and Namir shouted, *"Down,* Elza! Get down!" She did, and scuttled over to take one of the pistols.

A single answering bang came from the roof.

"Dustin's a good shot," Namir said. After a minute he stole up the stairs and cracked open the door to the roof. "Any luck?"

Dustin's response was inaudible, where we were. Namir came back down, still keeping low. "Target's not moving," he relayed. "Dead or wounded or playing possum. I guess Dustin doesn't want to use up a round, checking."

"Might be good strategy to shoot a couple," Paul said. "Make it look like we have ammo to spare."

"Might be. But I think the time for that is past, now. I better check out back."

"I'll go," Alba said. She had the riot gun. "Won't use this unless they're coming in the door."

"Good. Take the other pistol, Carmen." I did. It was the one Paul had used. Keep it in the family. I clicked the safety off, on, off again. A speck of red paint showed when it was off. Red equals fire, easy enough.

There was a long stammer of automatic fire, part of which crashed through the window. Only seven rounds of it, evidently;

there were seven small holes letting daylight in. But the glass hadn't shattered.

"He's close," Namir said in a hoarse whisper. "If Dustin can't see him, he's probably just behind the sandbags. Where you were on guard last night, Carmen."

I was trying to swallow, but couldn't. Most of those bullets hit the wall behind me. If I'd been standing up, I'd have been hit.

"Stay down," he said unnecessarily. "He might try to shoot out—" There was a longer sustained roar of fire, glass splintering everywhere, which blew a hole in the picture window more than two feet wide.

Namir stood up quickly and sighted through the hole. He stood still as a photograph for two seconds and then fired a single shot, which reverberated like a gong in the closed room.

"Lucky shot." He strode over to the front door, unbolted it, and opened it a couple of inches. He aimed down through the slit and fired once more.

"Okay. Paul, come check. Isn't this the guy from yesterday?"

I stepped over to look. It looked like him, Jemmie, in NASA coveralls, but he was face-down on the sidewalk, blood and brains sprayed in a fan from the back of his head; Namir's second shot. I swallowed bile.

He was still holding his weapon, a pistol not much bigger than mine, but with a large ammunition canister attached.

"Yeah," Paul said. "One to go, maybe?"

"I want to go up and take a look around. You cover things down here?"

"Sure." He didn't sound so sure.

Where would the third one be? Would he or she continue the plan alone? If I were in that situation, with the two others gone, I would be hiding now. Sneak away after the sun goes down.

Paul had said something to me. "What?"

"I want you to cover me while I run out and get that guy's gun. He has two magazines on his belt, too."

"Cover you? You mean shoot back if someone shoots at you?"

"Yeah. Keep their heads down."

"I only have five bullets in this thing."

"Here, trade." He set the rifle in front of me on the reception table, and took my pistol, ours.

He bounded out the door as I picked up the rifle. I barely had time to figure out the safety, when he came rushing back in with the weapon and its two magazines, and kicked the door shut with a slam behind him.

"Get down!" I was already crouching, but I flopped down, the rifle clattering under me, and there was a deafening explosion.

His face was about two feet from mine, and we stared at each other wild-eyed. "Grenade. Hand grenade."

Namir came rattling down the stairs. "What the fuck was that?"

"He had a hand grenade. I went out to get his weapon and I guess his hand relaxed. The whatchamacallit sprang off—"

"The arming lever."

"—and I just got back in time."

"God. That's why he shot out the hole in the window. To toss it in."

"I wonder if they have more," Paul said.

"I wonder why they had *one*!" Alba had crawled up with her shotgun. "Not exactly crowd control."

"Namir!" Dustin's voice from the door onto the roof. "Guy running away."

"Armed?"

"Not obviously."

He went up, taking two stairs at a time. I could hear them talking quietly, and then a single shot.

Namir came back down. "Shot over his head. Just let him know we saw him."

"Wonder if that's all of them," Alba said, standing up.

"Maybe there's one inside the building here," came a voice from the shadows. My brother Card came forward. He was holding one of the flare pistols, aimed at Alba.

"For God's sake, Card," Paul said, "don't shoot that thing indoors."

Alba set the shotgun on the floor and raised both her hands. "Let him have his say."

"You came out of the darkness with just what we needed. Guns, ammunition, information. You're pretty and smart and have a convincing and useful uniform. Anybody who's ever gamed knows that rule: If it seems to be too good to be true, it's probably not true."

"I have ID."

"I'm sure you do."

"It's a NASA ID with a DNA spot."

"Which means shit without electronics."

"Card," I said, "you're being paranoid."

"We all should be," he said. "Alba, even if you do work for NASA, or did, how do we know you're not one of them, now?"

Snowbird came up behind him. "I could speak to that," she said, "just from observation."

"What have you observed?" Card asked.

"This morning, when it became light, Alba could have taken the riot gun and killed everyone except the upstairs guard. And then, probably, killed the guard as soon as he opened the door. Her partners in this endeavor would be nearby—we know they were—and then the three of them would abduct me and get on with their plan."

"An idiotic idea to begin with," Alba said. "If, as you say, I'm smart, why would I team up with those idiots?"

"Good enough for me," Namir said. "Card, your caution is commendable. But excessive in this case, I think."

"I agree," Paul said. "The same thing occurred to me last night, Card. But after we'd talked for a while, no. Besides, she had plenty of opportunities last night and, as Snowbird said, this morning, and we're all still alive."

I saw a tense look pass between Paul and Namir, and could read it well: Paul was closer, and Namir's expression was saying, "You do it, and I'll be right behind you."

I opened my mouth to intervene, but then the totally unexpected happened.

"I'm sorry, Alba." Card lowered the gun. "I'm way out of line here. Forgive me?"

"Um . . . sure, Card." She slowly reached down and retrieved the shotgun.

"I'm used to spending most of my time in virtuality. Making my living in an imaginary world, and mostly living there. Without it, I suppose my imagination is a little out of control."

"It isn't a bad instinct," Namir said carefully. "We need to think in different ways; need to look at problems from every angle."

"Though we might stop short of pointing guns at each other," Paul said.

I was just plain stunned. The Card I grew up with would not have apologized if he'd caused the London Fire and 9/11 combined. The fifty years had mellowed him.

"Okay," Namir said. "If we're going to stay here much longer, we have to bury what's left of that poor bastard up front. He'll be smelling pretty bad by evening."

Something made the small hairs on the back of my neck stir. "Wait. Where's Meryl?"

Namir looked around. "Wasn't she with you?"

"Back in the kitchen, a minute ago." I called her name twice.

Dustin trotted back toward the kitchen. "Oh, shit," he said softly.

She was lying on the kitchen floor in front of the sink, her legs out straight, as if she were resting. There was a red stain the size of a playing card on the center of her chest and a large pool of blood under her back. The window over the sink had a bullet hole and blood spatter.

Dustin fell to his knees and tried to breathe life back into her.

I couldn't find breath myself. Elza shook her head, and said "No." She got down next to Dustin and grabbed his shoulders lightly. "That's not . . . She's too far gone."

Dustin didn't respond at first, but then eased the body back down. He wiped blood from his lips. "She didn't make a sound."

It was one of the bullets that had crashed through the living-room window. Paul and I found two spades in a shed out back. There was a patch of grass with some roses behind it. We all took turns standing guard and digging. After we buried her, Dustin said some words in Latin.

We washed up in the bathroom, avoiding the kitchen. The water from the tap was still warm.

I felt like part of me had died. I'd never been as close to Meryl as to the other five, but we had all lived through several different worlds together.

So we weren't immortal. We weren't even bulletproof.

"The hell with the body out front," Paul said. "Let's get our gear together and start pushing up to Fruit Farm."

"Nothing here for us," Namir said, then . . . "What the fuck?"

The lights had come back on.

✻

From *Rear View Mirror: an Immediate History,* by Lanny del Piche (Eugene, 2140):

. . . were the Others just playing a sadistic game, when they restored power temporarily on 30 April that year? If my guess is as good as anybody's, I'd say they were just temporarily changing the parameters of the experiment. Our physical comfort was of no concern to them, and our existential or psychological state was invisible, not even a variable.

My first area of study was animal behavior. We were reasonably enlightened in our treatment of test animals—any sign of cruelty or even lack of compassion would've resulted in student demonstrations and faculty censure.

But that was about animals who were cousins to humans. A lab rat shares more than our gross anatomical structure; it has more than hunger and thirst; it prefers one taste to another. Individual rats have individual personalities, even when they're raised in robotic unison. Sacrificing them was a necessary chore, but I remember how I grated my teeth when I grabbed one by the tail and swung him down to smack his head against the lab table. Did the other rats know what was going on? I don't remember them reacting; if they had, it would have upset me.

Perhaps a closer analogy would be in our study of microorganism cultures. A drop of nutrient doped with penicillin would create a clear circle that was the purposeful destruction of millions of creatures. And after their survivors had been measured and photographed, the whole small universe went into a red bio-waste bucket.

When the Others are done with us, will they leave us there on the table, to work out our individual and collective destinies?

Or will they be more fastidious than that . . .

# 5

We spread through the building, flipping light switches on and off. Suddenly, I heard a sustained musical note.

"What's that?"

"A-440," Namir said. "Like a tuning fork." We followed the sound to the Women's Lounge area, where a small cube had been left on.

"Same guy," Alba said. The one we called Spy—it couldn't be the same one literally; we'd left him twenty-five light-years away. Just a standard "human" interface for the Others.

He looked out of the cube, unblinking, for another minute or so. Then the tuning-fork sound ended, and he spoke:

"We have decided to give you power again, for one week, to see what happens." The screen went blank.

"One week," Paul said. "What do we do first?"

"Let's see if the cars work," Alba said. "One of those panel trucks, or a little bus."

I followed her out to the lot, carrying my superfluous pistol. Card came out, too. The morning was pleasant, still cool, about nine o'clock.

She got into the first car and punched in N-A-S-A on the dash keyboard.

"Shit." Faint numerals appeared on the windshield, ooh oom. "They probably all drained out."

We tried two others and got the same. Card found the recharging station and unreeled a cable out to a small bus. He plugged it into the rear.

"All right!" Alba called out from the driver's seat. She hopped down. "Is there another cable?"

"Two more. Maybe do that panel truck?" She looked at me and rubbed her chin. "Do you know how to drive?"

"Umm . . . it's been a while." I had a license back in 2070, but moved to Mars in '72. "Sixty-some years. I suppose cars are a lot different."

"But *you* can," she said to Card.

He shrugged. "I have a car, but I live in LA. Haven't touched a steering wheel in years."

"You may be about to." She pointed to a stolid-looking blocky sedan. "Might as well charge that one up, too. We may want to look official."

He went off to do that. "How long do they take to charge up?"

"An hour, maybe a couple of hours. Depends on the range,

mainly. And whether they're hooked up to free energy. You probably want to take the sedan to get the most miles."

"Couldn't fit Snowbird in there."

"Well, the panel truck, then." She pointed back at the building. Paul was at the door. "Carmen," he called, "we have a problem."

"Only one," Alba said. "How nice."

I went to him. "Snowbird's hurt. Another stray round hit her."

"How bad?"

"Who can say? She didn't even tell anybody about it; Dustin saw the hole."

We walked back to the snack area, where the Martian was standing in a corner. That was normal; she even slept standing up.

"It's a small thing, Carmen," she said. "Just a small bullet, which didn't hit any vital organs."

"Let me see." She turned around and showed me, a small black dot high on her back, about where a human shoulder would be. There was a little pink froth of blood.

"I can feel exactly where it is," she said. "It's not doing any harm."

Paul was standing behind me. "Are there any doctors for Martians at that Russian place?"

"There are members of the blue family. They're something like doctors."

"We have to get you there anyhow, for food. This just makes it a little higher priority."

"It's too far," she said.

"Not anymore," he said. "I'm a pilot. We just have to dig up an airplane somewhere."

"That would be a figure of speech?" Snowbird said. "They don't bury airplanes?"

"Right . . . Damn, I threw away my cell. Do you still have yours?"

"Think I can find it." I went into the next room, where we'd changed into NASA work clothes. My cell was in the corner where I'd tossed it, the power light a barely visible dull red. I plugged it into the wall and it went bright red, then yellow, then green. I took it in to Paul.

He punched a few numbers and shook his head. "Nothing's up and working yet, I suppose. Do you speak any Russian?"

"No, *nyet.*"

"I do," Snowbird said. "So does Namir. We used it sometimes on the starship."

I recalled that Namir's father had come from Russia. He'd gone back for some Olympics and brought home a souvenir balalaika, which was why our mysterious spy had such an odd instrument aboard a starship.

I took the phone from Namir and was looking at it, trying to decide what to do next, when it suddenly rang, the anonymous-caller tone. I punched the answer button, and a young woman's face appeared.

"Carmen Dula?" she said. "You look just like your picture!"

"Um . . . most people do."

"Sorry." She covered her eyes with a hand and winced. "I am Wednesday Parkman, calling from the office of the president. At Camp David, Maryland."

"Okay. What does the president want?"

"Well, I don't know, really. I was told to call your number and

Paul Collins's until one of you answered. But you answered right away. So let me try to find the president?"

"Sure, and Paul's here, too."

"Hold on!" Her face left, and we saw the ceiling for a moment, and then a slow pan of Monet's lilies, with a cello playing softly.

"I don't guess she's had this job for too long," I said.

"How the hell did they get up to Camp David without power?" Paul said.

"You couldn't walk there in a day," I said.

The lilies dissolved, replaced by an important-looking man I recognized just as he said his name. "Dr. Dula, I'm Morris Chambers. We met briefly at the White House."

"It seems like a long time ago."

"Doesn't it. The president is drawing together a committee to deal with the current"—he made a helpless gesture—"situation, and he'd like you to come here as soon as possible."

"Washington," Paul said, "or Camp David?"

"Washington is chaos," he said. "Once you're in the air, we'll give you a code word that will allow you to land at Camp David."

"Okay. So what do we get into the air with? We're still on the Armstrong Space Force Base."

"Let me check." He got up from the desk, and we had another minute of Monet and strings. He appeared again.

"You were rated for multi-engine commercial a half century ago. Airplanes are simpler now, but there's no GPS." Of course not, no satellites.

"If there are charts and a compass, I can sort it out. It would have computers, even without GPS?"

He looked away from the phone and then nodded. "Navigation computers, yes. There is a subsonic twelve-passenger NASA plane waiting for you on Runway 4, South terminal. That's the only secure terminal, they say, so go directly there. Security there wants your license-plate number."

Alba was leaning in the door. "Government plate, 21D272," she said. "It's a little blue bus." Paul repeated it.

"What will this committee be doing?" I asked. "What *can* they do in one week?"

"The key phrase is 'maximum survival.' We estimate that there are still about 300 million people alive in America after yesterday. We would like to have . . . a maximum still alive a year from now. Having learned how to live without technology."

"It won't be 300 million," Paul said. "It won't even be 100 million."

The bureaucrat's face didn't change. "You understand what we're facing. It will be a disaster of biblical scope no matter what we do. We do want to maximize the number who survive, but we also want to preserve a semblance of the American way of life."

Paul nodded. "That will be interesting. I'll call you next from the airplane." He closed the phone and handed it back to me. "Cheeseburgers and idiotic television? I wonder what the American way of life *is* nowadays."

"If they really want maximum survival," Namir said, "they're aiming for a totally protective welfare state that's also a police state. Which identifies the ones chosen to survive, and lets the rest go find some way to die. Or is there some humane alternative?"

"We have plenty of time to talk about it en route. We'll be in the air most of the day."

"Slow plane?" Alba said.

Namir nodded slowly. "We'll be going by way of Russia, of course. They'd never allow us to take Snowbird there if we went to Camp David first."

"Of course. Over the Pole," I said. Hoping the Others don't decide to turn off the power prematurely.

We loaded the bus in a hurry, deciding to hold on to all the food and weapons. We could use up the perishables on the way to Camp David, and the rest might come in handy next week.

Alba did the driving; she knew the way, and nobody else but Card had driven during this century. Leaving the place, we passed a sight I could have lived without, a trio of buzzards tearing up the body on the sidewalk. Paul winced at the sight but didn't say anything.

The guards at the airfield gate knew Alba, of course, and waved us through. There were a couple of dozen planes parked around, but she followed a line painted on the tarmac that led to Runway 4, where a woman was standing by a small passenger plane.

One problem was immediately manifest: you got into the plane by climbing a narrow set of stairs that led to a narrow door—not wide enough for a Martian. Fortunately, the baggage compartment was pressurized, and the bay was a couple of meters wide. The ramp going up to it was a conveyor belt; she gave a thumping Martian laugh as she rolled up.

Paul was talking to the woman while this was going on. She was a flight controller who also flew, but she'd never piloted one this big, and she'd never flown without GPS. Paul hadn't either, in a real-life situation, but in Space Force training he'd flown everything from gliders to spaceships. By the seat of his pants, as they say.

They went up into the cockpit and checked out the emergency navigation system, which could work by compass headings and a VR cube that showed what the ground looked like from any altitude over any place on Earth. Goggles that could see through clouds.

It only took a few minutes to load up our provisions and weaponry. "Well," Alba said, "I guess I'll be leaving you now."

"Not if you don't want to," Paul said, looking down the aisle of the plane. "This is an alien planet to us; you and Card are our native guides. You know modern weapons, and the riot gun doesn't work for anyone else."

Everybody murmured or nodded assent, even me. Though I didn't care for the way he carefully didn't look at her when he knew I was watching.

Well, we've always given each other that freedom. But neither of us had exercised it in some years. Not to mention light-years.

The plane started taxiing, and there was some discussion over the radio when Paul turned left. For some reason, they thought we were going east. We took off headed for the North Pole.

In retrospect, I suppose they had the ability and authority to shoot us down. I'm glad I didn't think of that until later.

The ride was pretty bumpy and loud until we got to cruising altitude. Then it was just a mild vibration, with the noise from the wind and engine canceled out.

Alba came up the aisle and sat next to me, offering to share a packet of nuts and dried fruit.

"This may seem funny," she said, "but I'm not quite clear on what you and Paul actually did. I mean, I was never good at history. That was like forty years before I was born."

Fair enough. What did I know about 2014, forty years before I was born? Had they started building the space elevator yet? I'd have to look it up.

# 6

"It kind of started with the space elevator. Our family—Card and me and our parents—won a sort of lottery. There was a small colony on Mars, mostly single scientists, that wanted to start accepting families.

"So we took the space elevator up to orbit—two pretty boring weeks—and then got on an old-fashioned spaceship to Mars. That was most of a year, but it wasn't boring. I started college, VR to the University of Maryland, and met Paul, and we fell in love."

"He was a lot older than you?"

"Well, yeah, I'd just turned nineteen and he was thirty-one. But it worked out."

"I can see."

How sweet. "Well, it caused no end of trouble with the administration of Mars, namely one walking disaster, Dargo Solingen. She clearly disapproved, and did everything she could to keep us apart."

"Which had the opposite effect, I suppose."

"That's for sure. Well, we'd been in Mars, as they say, for little more than a year, and she caught me in an unforgivable situation, swimming with a bunch of other kids in a new water tank. Since I was the oldest, she rained all kinds of shit on me. Including barring me from the surface.

"Well, that didn't last. I snuck out after midnight, planning to walk a couple of kilometers and come straight back—Card had figured out how to disable the alarm on the air lock.

"But I had an accident. Crossed a place where the crust was eggshell-thin and fell some distance to the floor of a lava tube.

"I broke my ankle, and that should've been the end of it. Nobody knew where I was, and the radio didn't work."

"Which was when the Martians came to the rescue. I remember that."

"One Martian, anyhow, the one we called Red. They all look pretty much the same, at least to us, but they wear different colors according to their family. Red was the only one who wore red."

"Of course I know about him."

"Everyone should. Anyhow, he collected me and flew me back to their underground city, where they used some kind of mumbo-jumbo medical science to fix my ankle.

"It did occur to me to wonder why these weird-looking aliens should be living in an earthlike environment in a huge pressurized cave under the Martian surface. I asked Red, and he said he didn't know, and at the time I wondered whether he was holding something back. He wasn't; it was a mystery to them as well."

"They didn't know they'd been built by the Others," Alba said.

"Yes and no. They had a tradition, almost mystical, that the Others had created them and brought them from someplace unimaginably far away. When they first told us about that, it sounded like a creation myth. But it was literally true, and explained a lot."

"Like how they had this high-tech life but knew nothing about science."

"Right. You know about the Martian pulmonary cysts?"

"The Martian lung crap, yeah."

"That's what brought us together, Martians and humans. Nobody believed my story about these Martians living in a cave—well, my mother almost believed—but then everybody under about the age of twenty caught the lung crap. I'd brought the spores back with me."

"So Red showed up with the cure."

"In essence, yes. And the humans and Martians started studying each other.

"Well, the Martians had been studying *us* for a century and a half, listening to our radio broadcasts and watching flatscreen and cube. They'd learned ten or twelve human languages over the years.

"They told us about the Others, but we dismissed it as mythmaking, a kind of religion—you know, these almighty beings gave birth to us a jillion years ago."

"And then you found out it was literally true."

"That's right." The yellow family, the ones who wore only yellow, specialized in memory, and they swore that the memory of the Others was real. It was vague and patchy because it was tens of thousands of years old, but it wasn't a myth.

"Then, in 2079, the Others proved it. A signal that triggered strange behavior in the yellow family. They started babbling weird nonsense—but they each said the same nonsense over and over. Turned out to be a binary code that basically told us who the Others were and what their body chemistry was, nitrogen and silicon. They lived in liquid nitrogen, and this one—there was only one in the solar system—lived in a liquid-nitrogen sea on Triton, Neptune's moon. It had lived there for twenty-seven thousand years.

"Once we cracked the code and tried to communicate with it, we found out that it spoke English. And Chinese and German and whatever."

"But they couldn't just call and say hello?"

"No. It was like a series of tests, to see how sophisticated we could be. The first test was contact with the Martians, and in fact was why the Martians were there."

"I understand that one. It was like a signal to the Others that we had gone to another planet. Which woke up the one on Triton. But it woke up knowing how to speak Chinese and all?"

"We don't think so. We think it absorbed a huge amount of information from the yellow family as soon as it woke up. At least that's what the Martians say.

"The last test was playing for keeps. We were in Earth orbit, and Red found out that he was essentially a time bomb. In a couple of days, he would explode, giving out more energy than the Sun. The seas underneath us would boil; the air would be blown away. I guess you know what happened then."

She nodded gravely. "Paul took Red to the other side of the Moon, so when he blew up, the earth wasn't hurt."

"That's right, and perhaps if we had left it at that, everything would be fine. The Other that had been on Triton blew it up and went home to Wolf 25, almost twenty-five light-years from here."

"But we had to follow it."

"There were various opinions. A lot of people wanted to build a war fleet and go after the bastards, which was not really possible, even with free energy."

"It's always been free for me," Alba said. I hadn't thought of that. "Go on?"

"Well, at the other extreme were people who just wanted to say 'good riddance,' and get on with life. I have a lot of sympathy for that idea.

"There was a lot of arguing that eventually wound up with the compromise that started, I guess, before your parents were born."

"My mother was born in 2090."

"Two years after we launched. Well, the bright idea was to build one starship, and send it off to Wolf 25 on a peace mission."

"But then they also built a fleet here in orbit, supposedly to protect the earth."

"Or at least to mollify the hawks," I said, "the ones who demanded a military response. But it was gnats versus an elephant."

"I know a lot of people who thought it was a bad idea," Alba said. "Almost all my teachers in school."

"I can imagine. We had a kind of meeting with one of the Others, who showed us evidence of what they could do, as if a further demonstration was necessary. Did you hear what they did to their own home planet?"

"Yeah, I saw that on the cube. How they used to be, well, not human but sort of. But they evolved themselves into these ice-cold monsters who lived on a frozen moon. So they came back and destroyed their own home planet?"

"In self-defense, they pointed out. They showed us the remains of the fleet that the home planet had been building to attack them. Sort of like our fleet here, but a thousand times closer.

"So we came back and, in essence, brought the eyes and ears of the Others with us. That was the human-looking avatar that was on the cube.

"And so they blew up the Moon to keep us out of space. We tried anyhow, and so they pulled the plug on civilization."

She nodded, thoughtful. "They could have just killed us."

"I'm sure they still have that option. You have to remember that this was all preplanned. The Others can't beat the speed of light; it will be almost twenty-five years before they actually know of the fleet, and twenty-five more before they could come back and do something about it. So all of their actions—blowing up the Moon, turning off the free power—have been in place for a long time."

"Like booby traps, waiting for us to set them off."

"That's right. And who's to say they don't have another one, waiting to blow us off the face of the earth if we misbehave?"

"Or put everything back the way it was, if we don't."

I laughed. "They're not putting the Moon back together."

"You don't know. Maybe they could."

I started to say something about increasing entropy, but let it go. Hell, maybe they could track down all the pieces and rebuild the Moon. And then turn it into green cheese.

# 7

The landing at Novosibirsk was delayed for an hour while they waited for the afternoon sun to melt the ice off the runway. When we got off the plane finally, there was a small crowd waiting, dozens of people and seven Martians. It wasn't too cold, about noon, bright sun in a deep blue sky. We hurried inside anyhow.

Two of the Martians, the ones in blue, wanted to hustle Snowbird away and start working on her injury. She made them wait while she said good-bye and thanked us individually.

"When I first saw you," she said to me, "you were also injured, stranded on an alien planet. I hope I do as well as you." She gestured at one of the blue ones. "We even have the same doctor."

The blue one nodded at me. "I fixed your ankle sixty-four years ago."

"Don't do everything he says," I said to Snowbird. "He's pretty old." She favored me with a thumping laugh and was gone.

The Russians couldn't let us go without eating. Namir answered their questions about what we knew about the rest of the world while they feasted us on thin pancakes rolled around sour cream and pungent caviar, washed down with icy vodka. The last such meal we would ever have, I assumed. When the power went back off, we would be stranded somewhere, presumably far from caviar.

We got back on the plane, and Paul tried to raise Camp David. A signal was coming through, but it was unintelligible. We charted a course over the Arctic and took off, slithering a bit on the slush that was forming on the runway.

While we flew south, Dustin took over a little study carrel in the rear of the plane and tried to find out what had happened to Fruit Farm, the Oregon commune where he'd grown up.

It was still there physically, if it had survived the Martian abdication. Maybe it was better off than most places, being totally independent of the power and communications grid.

More than a decade before the Martian free power (the year that Dustin's family left the commune) they had declared total independence, and shut themselves off from the outside world. They had low-voltage solar power and two wind machines, and an environment that allowed year-round subsistence agriculture.

Recent satellite photos showed a tall stockade enclosing about eighty acres of orderly plats around a village of about a hundred people. Outside the stockade were fruit orchards and fields of grain.

One day a year, the vernal equinox, Fruit Farm was open to the public. They sold organic produce and gave tours of their utopian compound. At sundown, they closed the doors for another year. They did maintain an organic produce stand outside the stockade.

It wasn't a totally hermetic existence. Individuals and families were allowed to join the commune if they had useful skills, and there always was a waiting list. Dustin's family had spent eight years there, and he looked forward to visiting. If the place still existed, after the past week's troubles.

The twelve passenger seats unfolded into lumpy beds, angled like chevrons. Some of us rested or napped. Paul took a pill. The plane was on autopilot, but if the Others turned off the power we'd be on a glider looking for a flat place to land.

We were over Hudson Bay, after about six hours, when we made contact with the president's people. I couldn't hear what was going on, but I presumed they were livid. They gave us a plane and we hijacked it to Russia. Paul was grinning broadly as he gave them monosyllabic replies.

The Northeast was greener than I'd expected. Big cities and crowded exurbs, but a lot of forest, too. Broad superhighways with almost no traffic. Occasional knots of pileups, dozens or even hundreds of abandoned cars.

When we were a couple of hundred miles from Camp David, we were joined by a pair of military jets that moved in close enough to make eye contact. Paul waved and one of them waved back, and they banked off and sped away.

Namir noted that the day's travel had reduced our fuel supply from 0.97 to 0.95. We could go around the world fifty times if we wanted to.

"Let's hope this thing is productive," I said, without high hopes.

The president must have been the genius who had authorized the rocket launch through the meteor storm, which had so pissed off the Others. But he presumably was the best person to organize a nationwide response to prepare for the coming dark age.

We landed without incident, and Paul followed directions, taxiing us to a reviewing stand. A lot of people in suits, squinting into the morning sun. No brass band.

Spatters of applause as we stepped down in random order. Alba grinned broadly when the applause faltered. Who the hell was she?

We were seated on folding chairs, and a couple of soldiers armed with boxed lunches came out. Room-temperature tuna-salad sandwiches. Not caviar, but I was hungry.

I scanned the faces of the dignitaries and was a little disappointed not to see President Gold. Then someone introduced President Boyer. A gaunt man in his fifties approached the microphone.

"He was vice president," Alba whispered. "Something must have happened to Gold."

The new president greeted us and bloviated for a few minutes about the importance of our "mission."

It was two-pronged: try to repair some of the damage done by the power outage and meanwhile try to tool up for a nineteenth-century life style. Either one clearly impossible in a week. But we had to do something.

Factories that could be converted were already cranking out carts and bicycles and hand plows and cargo wagons—a pity horses and oxen couldn't be mass-produced. This brave new world would be largely powered by human muscle—from humans who had been free from the necessity of physical labor for generations.

A lot of time and effort were being spent, perhaps wasted, trying to figure out how to preserve a central government without modern communication. It seemed obvious that you couldn't, given the size of the country and the time lag between decision and response. You weren't going to have Ben Franklin closing up his print shop and taking off for the Continental Congress on foot. Or mule or whatever.

We followed the president and the seven others who had been on stage with him up a gravel path to a large rustic lodge, old log walls and a slate roof. There were other buildings around that looked equally old and homespun.

"This is the main lodge," the president said as he went up the timber stairs to the porch. "It goes back almost two hundred years. Franklin Roosevelt in World War II."

Pretty old for a wooden building, I thought, but there was probably a lot of technology embedded in its reassuring simplicity.

"Let's go down to the planning room. You space travelers, I want to talk to you first. You have a unique point of view. President Gold, before he died, told me to take full advantage of that." We followed them down a spiral staircase into a well-lit room that was twenty-second-century neo-Baroque.

The room was dominated by a heavy ornate round table of some gorgeous rare wood. There were about twenty overstuffed swivel chairs with twenty different colors of paisley upholstery. The latest thing, I supposed.

There were five of us "space travelers" and our two hangers-on, facing seven people who were presumably politicians.

An impressive back-lit Mercator projection of the world filled one wall. Namir gestured at it as we sat down. "Please bring us up to date . . . next week, that whole map is going to be of only academic interest. What are we doing to make people adjust to thinking and acting on a small scale? Local government and industry?"

"Right now we're still dealing with panic. Rioting and wholesale looting." That was Dali Spendor, who had been President Gold's press secretary. "That requires local response, but it's military and police work."

"National Guard?" Paul said. Some of the others looked bewildered.

"There's no such thing anymore," General Ballard said. "It seemed obsolete, and was absorbed by the regular military before I was ever a soldier."

"Regionalism in general has been on the wane." A white-bearded man who introduced himself as Julian Remnick, president of Harvard University. "That's been true for centuries. But facing a common enemy as terrifying as the Others, who represent the same danger to everyone from Nome to Key West, from London to Beijing, has unified the world more effectively than millennia of idealism." He was obviously quoting himself. "That has its bad side now."

"People will naturally expect a top-down response," Spendor said. "Here, that would be Washington stepping in to deal with the problem. But as Namir says, that stops on Wednesday."

"Or sooner," I said. "There's no reason to trust the Others' word on anything."

"Nothing we can do about that," the president huffed. Except try to be flexible, I thought, which probably wasn't his strong suit.

"We've started to make a little progress," a tall plain woman said. "I'm Lorena Monel, governor of Maryland. Or former governor. As you say, units as large as a state will probably have little meaning.

"My committee on localization has gotten in touch with regional leaders in both major parties, and two other groups that represent significant numbers. Through them, we've made contact with thousands of community leaders and put them together in an information net—useless after the power goes off, but meanwhile they're talking with people who will be within walking distance. Leaders with the same regional resources and problems."

"In Wyoming," a slender tanned fellow drawled, "ain't nobody in walking distance of nobody else. Except in the cities, and they're pretty well lost."

"There won't *be* anyone in Wyoming by the end of the week," the president said. "No one but hermits. You going back?"

The man stared back at him. "Good a place to die as any."

"Let's get back on track," the Maryland governor said. "We have this network for five days. How can we best use it?"

"Turn it into a cell system," the Harvard president said. "Have each community establish a line of communication with every adjacent one, through Lorena's committee. Have each of them figure out a way to stay in contact with their immediate neighbors without high technology."

"Smoke signals," the Wyoming man said.

"Possibly. Signal fires, anyhow. The ancient Greeks did that."

"Horses and riders?" I said. "Are there enough people who still do that?"

"Wouldn't work if they did," a short black man said. "Jerry Fenene, deputy secretary of commerce. In a couple of weeks, a horse isn't going to be transportation. It's going to be a million calories on the hoof. You don't want to ride it anywhere near a hungry person with a gun."

"Bicycles are a near equivalent," the president said (giving me a vision of someone eating a bicycle), "and we're churning them out. Twenty-four-hour production in, I don't know, a couple of hundred factories."

"A hundred eighty-two registered," Fenene said. "Some of them very small. They might turn out a hundred thousand bikes before the power goes." He shook his head. "It's not of much practical significance. There must be a hundred million bikes out there already." He looked vaguely in our direction.

I wondered what they expected us to do, to help. We were public figures in a way, but most of the public associated us with getting *into* this disaster, not getting out.

We did have more experience with the Others, but in terms of actual contact, that was a matter of minutes, not much of it constructive. Lab rats probably knew more about humans than we knew about the Others. And had more in common with their captors.

"No matter what we do," the president said, "it's just a drop in a mighty big bucket. They give us a week, now less than six days." He looked at me. "If that. Once we have your cell system, Lorena, what do we do with it?"

"I guess the next step would be to organize groups of cells. Into regions. How big would a region be?"

"Smaller than Wyoming," I said, "if you want meetings."

"You can bike across Wyoming," the thin man said, "but you wouldn't want to."

"I don't like this assumption that everybody's going to cooperate," Namir said. "Line up and form into counties and states. With no central authority, I'd put my money behind mob rule. Gangs, with the biggest bully at the top."

"You're always such a crazy optimist," Paul said.

"So what would *you* bet on?"

He scratched his head. "Same."

"So I should be the biggest bully?" the president said. "I probably have the biggest gang."

"The only one with nukes and hellbombs," Wyoming said, and some people laughed nervously. "You could just wait it out," he continued. "Let the rest of the world go to hell first, and then come out when the smoke clears."

"Give up on America?" the president said. "There's no way I could do that."

"That's not America out there anymore." Wyoming made a sweeping gesture. "When the power goes off again, it's gonna be one big nut house, with the inmates armed and desperate—and in charge. Let them take care of each other."

Namir spoke quietly into the silence: "How many troops do you have? I mean here at Camp David."

The president looked at General Ballard. "The Secret Service right here, that might be sixty-some agents?" Ballard said. "The First Brigade of the 101st is attached to them, but I don't think there were a hundred on duty in and around the White House when we . . . evacuated. My adjunct, Brigadier Akers, would have the exact number. Under two hundred total."

"So we're spread out pretty thin," Namir said, "if a group of any size decides to attack us."

The general laughed, a hoarse syllable. "We're armed to the teeth, and those troops are the cream. No bunch of civilian rabble is going to breach our perimeter."

"Armed to the teeth with modern weapons." Namir shook his head. "You even have combat aircraft and tanks. Which all will be useless scrap after Wednesday. And we'll have a ring of a hundred-some soldiers with rifle-clubs and knives. If they do have knives. Excuse me if I want to be someplace less conspicuous."

"This is what it boils down to," Wyoming said. "Eight billion people had enough to eat last week, but about seven billion need agribusiness and large-scale aquaculture to stay alive. Nothing you do is going to change those seven billion into small-scale farmers and fishers. Even if you could, the Earth wouldn't support them. Long before winter comes, there won't be any food on the shelves. No grain in the silos."

"There's no way around it," Namir said, "if the Others pull the plug on agribusiness. So most of those seven billion have to die."

"Some'll be food themselves," Wyoming said. "One adult has what, forty or fifty pounds of meat on him? Keep you goin' for a month and a half."

"If you had refrigeration," Paul said.

"Or know how to make jerky," Wyoming said, giving Paul a measuring stare. Probably two months' worth.

"But it's not like a lifeboat situation," I said, "where you draw straws, or the strong eat the weak. At least in America, there's plenty of room to hole up and wait."

"We can impose order for a certain length of time," the president said. "In most cities, food warehouses and supermarkets are under armed guard."

"Unless the mobs have overpowered them," Lorena said. "I know that it hasn't worked in Baltimore, where my office is. The guard evaporated everywhere, and every crumb of food was gone by noon yesterday. When the power came back on, some people were ready. They used trucks to smash into stores and loot them wholesale. In a couple of cases, military units themselves did the looting, or at least joined the looters."

"We should assume the worst," Namir said, "and plan in terms of rebuilding from whatever ruins are left. Some countries have more experience in that than others." There was always the echo of Gehenna in his voice, in his accent. All his family dead in minutes. Cities paved with instant corpses. Israel had rebuilt, after a fashion, but never recovered.

"A basic question," Paul said to the president. "Are there federal reserves of food? Something that will still be there after the smoke clears?"

"In fact, there is." He pursed his lips and paused, and then continued. "Not too far from here, in a natural limestone cave in West Virginia. The Congress is holed up there, along with I don't know how many tons of cheese and freeze-dried milk and fruit and meat. Bought up in secret from individual states' surpluses, back in the Marlowe administration. The soldiers who are guarding it don't know what's there; they think it's a secret missile site. It can feed tens of thousands of people for decades—or could. With trucks to move it out."

"That's where you'll go after Camp David dries up?" Namir asked. The president reddened and looked away.

"Won't do much for the country in general," Paul said, "or the world."

"We're still six months away from winter," Namir said. Most of those billions will be dead by then. Unless they all move to Wyoming and start eating each other.

"The ones who survive the winter will provide the core for rebuilding the countries in the northern hemisphere. We should be working on what to do then. How to keep civilization going with those millions."

"Civilization is what got us here," Dustin said. "Maybe we should try something else."

"This isn't a philosophy problem, Professor."

"Except that everything is. In the long run, we might find that civilization is incompatible with survival."

"In the long run, that'll take care of itself," Wyoming said.

"It will not," Dustin pressed on. "Look, I grew up in a small, isolated, agrarian community that was founded in opposition to commercialism. I do know what I'm talking about; I was perfectly happy, absent most of civilization's overrated virtues.

"But it didn't just happen, and it certainly can't happen in the barbaric chaos you're all accepting as inevitable."

"You can't beat the math, boy. Nobody's gonna lay down and die so you and your pals can get naked and grow vegetables."

"I know that. That's why the organization initially has to come from here. We have some idea of where the food is and where the people are. For a few days, we can put that knowledge to use and maximize the number of people who live."

"Tell everybody where the food is," Namir said, "so they can loot more efficiently."

"It's a choice between triage and random survival," Paul said. "Only a billion are going to survive, and all you're really saying is that we might have some choice as to which billion."

"No, I'm just saying we can maximize the number," the president said. "There will be something like natural selection going on, but it won't be a matter of brute force. Quite the opposite, I think. People who cooperate with one another."

"People who obey the government." Wyoming said *gummint*. "Sometimes I think you boys made this whole thing up, Boyer. Mr. President."

The phone in front of General Ballard buzzed and he snatched it up. "Ballard, go."

The president set down his knife and fork and looked at Ballard. They both seemed to have gone a little pale. It wouldn't be a routine call—"How's supper with the prez?"

Ballard said, "I'm coming," and stood up. "Sir, there is, um, a disturbance on the east slope." He tossed his napkin down.

"What kind of 'disturbance'?"

"I don't know. Gunfire, on the other side of the fence. A sniper, at least one, silent. If you'll excuse me." Two other military guys followed him.

The woman with the sergeant's stripes and apron came out, armed with a wooden spoon. "Mr. President, shall I show people down to the basement?"

"Yes, thank you. Um . . . military people stay up here, of course, and you space folks?"

"Sure," Paul said. "Half of us are some sort of military anyhow."

"I'll stay, too," Card said to me. "You'll need an innocent bystander."

The cook-sergeant told the civilians to bring their plates and wineglasses if they wanted; they'd be hiding in the wine cellar. They were nervous but animated, a little jovial, as they filed out.

The president nodded and steepled his fingers under his chin. "There is a large safe room underneath the basement. Don't think we need it yet. Jorge, go where the general's going and send us a cube." One of the waiters flung the folded napkin off his arm and hustled toward the door. A pistol appeared in his hand as he was leaving the room. "Uncle Charlie, stand by the dome?" The other waiter nodded and left.

"We're pretty well protected here," he said to the dinner table. "If we turn on the pressor dome, a fly couldn't get in. Nor any missile. But we'd lose communication with outside, and probably fry everyone's personal electronics."

"And it would stop working on Wednesday," Namir said.

"I assume so. I'm not a scientist." I'm not either, but it did sound like a safe bet. Even if the pressor field wasn't itself electronic—I didn't know anything about it, but remembered that it was something like the "weak action force," as basic as gravity. But it must have some parts that plug into the wall.

"Without the pressor field," Namir said, "we'd still be safe down-stairs?"

He nodded. "It goes back at least to the twenty-first. There was probably a shelter down there in Eisenhower's day. They had nukes back then, too."

"A wonder we've lasted this long," Elza said. The president nodded, immune to sarcasm. Or maybe he knew something we didn't. Some presidential secret, whispered down from one to the next for three-hundred-some years. Except for the assassinations.

"Maybe we ought to go down there," I said.

"I don't know." The president used his napkin to wipe sweat from his forehead. "I'm afraid there are electronic locks on the exits. We couldn't hide indefinitely."

"Trapped in the darkness," Dustin said. "Airless. No, thanks."

A section of a book-lined wall rotated to reveal a large cube, about six feet square by two feet deep. The picture was bouncing; evidently Jorge was trying to image the scene as he ran toward it. Helmet cam, probably.

The image was pale green, with white flares when a couple of soldiers fired rifles.

"I wonder who they are," I said. "The people attacking."

"If they're the ones we were expecting, it's a bunch led by the Liberty Bell underground. They were trying to organize something down in Frederick, Maryland. We had a woman planted in their leadership, but we stopped hearing from her yesterday morning."

"How many?" Namir said.

"Three hundred, maybe four."

"Why don't they wait till after Wednesday?" I asked. "Wouldn't they know that most of the soldiers have electric guns?"

"Most of them do, too. Civilian hunting rifles. They're probably holding their gunpowder weapons in reserve until after the power goes off." There was the thunk-thunk sound of a heavy machine gun, and the cube showed it was on our side. "We should, too."

"This probably isn't the real attack," Namir said thoughtfully. "May just be a probe, to test your reaction."

"That's what you'd do?"

"I wouldn't attack a fortified position in any case, unless it had something I really wanted. Like the president."

He laughed. "Fat lot of good I'll be after the communications go out."

"They want you before that."

"Suppose so. Though I'm not sure what they'd do with me. Trade me for food?"

"Maybe they just want Camp David," he said. "Easy to defend without electricity, and all that meadowland would be good for planting. A fortified farm like Dustin's bunch."

"My 'bunch' doesn't have much winter," Dustin pointed out. "This place probably gets a lot of snow."

The president nodded. "Gold used to come up on weekends for cross-country skiing. That was a circus."

There were three loud, evenly spaced impacts on the log wall, like heavy sledgehammer blows.

"What was that?" Namir said.

The president shrugged and looked at one of the guards. "Sir," he said, "it sounds like a large-caliber air rifle, a sniper gun. No report because the ball goes slower than sound. I'd stay away from the windows, sirs."

We all moved toward the wall in between the two west windows. This was where the Indians would start shooting flaming arrows. Ride in looping orbits until the inferno forced us out.

"Shit," Paul said, "we shouldn't have left the guns on the plane."

"Some downstairs," the president said. He strode over to a door in the corner and thumbed the lock open. "Backup weapons for the army, I guess. On a rifle rack in the hall."

Namir jerked his head in that direction, and all five of us crept over, staying close to the wall. I didn't care for the idea of joining the president's army, but being an unarmed target was ridiculous.

As we clattered down the metal stairs, I felt panic rising, and a kind of helpless anger. A week ago, Earth was a beautiful blue marble floating in space, full of promise. The surface, it was nothing but fear and panic.

We used to joke about that. Most of my adult life has been in and on Mars, and her two moons were named fear and panic, Phobos and Diemos. When they rose or set together, we'd sometimes gather in the dome and watch. Drinking bad sweet Martian wine or worse brandy. It was a good place to live, toasting fear and panic. I hoped it still was. I had grandchildren there, old enough to vote.

I stood on the concrete floor numb, while Namir and Paul and Dustin smashed open the glass case and shouted about which weapons to take. It all seemed in slow motion. Great-grandchildren? My children, my twins, were born in '84. They'd be fifty-four Earth years old by now, twenty-eight Martian ares. They could have married at ten, and yes, their children might have children. I hadn't thought to ask.

Paul thrust a lightweight laser weapon into my arms, rather than a mewling infant, so my career as a great-grandmother was over after a second and a half.

I followed him up the stairs, almost tripping, because I was looking at the weapon rather than my feet. The safety was an on/off switch just above where your right thumb rested when your finger was on the trigger. A line of light on the top of the shoulder stock showed how much charge was left. Mine was halfway up, amber in color. Enough to fry an egg? A person?

Paul whispered, "I'll go check the plane," and slipped out the back door, before I could say anything. He had his rifle and two bandoliers of ammunition, but not even a hat against the rain.

The two guards were kneeling by both the windows. I sat down next to one of them, and we exchanged nods. "Anything?"

He shook his head no and squinted outside for a moment, then jerked back. Of course you wouldn't want to stay silhouetted long enough for that sniper to aim at you.

Alba crouched next to the soldier. "Are you in contact with the ones outside?"

He tapped his ear. "Yeah, but radio silence," he whispered. "They're out past the wire."

Alba's weapon was the same as mine. She pushed a button on the end of the stock and a long silver fuel cell came out. She licked her thumb and rubbed both the terminals, and slid it back into place with a quiet click.

The president was sitting on a worn leather couch in the corner farthest away from doors and windows. Hiding inside a bulky bulletproof vest and a heavy military helmet, he looked kind of ridiculous, like a boy playing soldier. He was punching buttons on what looked like an oversized phone, perhaps dictating the fate of the Free World. Such of it as remained.

After a long time, I looked at the clock on the wall behind me. It was 1:45; maybe ten minutes had passed. How long were we going to sit here listening to the rain?

I remembered Namir's refrain, "I will not quit my post until properly relieved." Would soldiers wait patiently through old age and into dust while their leaders forgot about them? Not a sound from outside except the oscillating swish of rain being pushed by wind.

The soldier touched his throat. "Sitrep?" he whispered. "Tony?" He cupped a hand over his ear, and then shrugged at Alba. I guess I didn't look military enough to shrug at.

The green picture on the cube shifted, sliding around about 180 degrees; Jorge looking back at us. The old lodge was a faint outline against the trees, our dark windows showing as light squares in the storm's gloom. From heat, I suppose. Cold as it was in here.

There was some machine-gun fire, farther away, answered by the crackling of laser fire as it popped rain. "Maybe some of them are falling back," the soldier said. "Or maybe it's just a bluff, a diversion," he stage-whispered to the other soldier. "What do you think, Boog?"

"I'm a sergeant," he said. "They don't pay me to think."

"Give it a try."

"I guess they figured to pop a few rounds to keep us awake all night. Then they go rest and come hit us when we're tired."

"That sounds right," Namir said, sitting next to the soldier who had spoken. "That's their big tactical advantage. Even if we outgun them, they control when and where we fight."

"Unless we take it to them," the first one said. "Maybe that's what they're doing now, chasing them."

"Leaving us alone here? I don't think so."

Not alone, of course. We also have a relatively useless president and a handful of intrepid interstellar space explorers. What are a few hundred people with guns against six who've faced the Others and lived to tell the tale? And a seventh who was able to walk through darkness undetected? Plus a zombie brother who had lost two of his three lives. Who could blame the rabble for running?

"A lot depends on how many of their weapons are electrical," Namir said. "They must know that the military have powder weapons."

"They might also know that our powder ammunition would be used up after a few minutes of heavy fighting. They might've been stockpiling reloads for years."

"What is a reload?" I asked.

"It's a do-it-yourself recycling thing," the other soldier said. "You save your empty cartridges and refill them with lead and powder. Tax on ammo is really high." He looked at Namir. "Was there a lot of ammo down there?"

He shook his head slowly and bit his lip, thinking. "We emptied a green metal box that had, what, ten bandoliers, maybe twelve. There were three other boxes." Like Paul, he had two bandoliers slung over his shoulders, across his chest, looking like a dangerous Mexican *bandito*.

"Bandolier's got 240 rounds," the soldier said, "twenty cartons. Hope there's more."

The back door swung open, and Paul clumped in, dripping. "Plane looks okay," he said, pressing water from his hair. He cut a glance toward the kitchen door. "Coffee."

I followed him into the kitchen; Namir and Elza followed me. Paul grabbed a tea towel to wipe off his rifle.

"Look, this is bad. The plane's okay right now because you have to cross so much exposed ground to get to it. But once they flank this building, they can hit it with gunfire. One lucky shot would disable it."

"So let's get the hell out of here," Namir said, "while the plane still works. They're gonna rest up tomorrow, and then on Wednesday it'll be Custer surrounded by the Sioux." I didn't quite know what that meant, but was sure it was nothing good.

"We should go right now," Elza said. "Every minute we stay here—"

"Take me with you." The president had slipped quietly into the kitchen behind us.

Paul looked at him. "Rather take two of the soldiers."

"What?" He seemed surprised. "But I can be . . . I'm the president."

"What did you do to Professor Gold?"

"Gold was an old man. The shock of the last few days, the Others . . . it was more than his heart could take."

"Bullshit. I talked with him the day before he died. He was fine."

"But old."

"He swam a half mile a day to relax. He didn't have a heart attack."

"He did, though. I was there."

Paul looked at him for a long moment. "Go tell the soldiers we're going to take you to safety. Ask them to cover us. Then we'll make a break for it."

He shook his head. "What if . . ."

"I'll go get the others," I said, and walked by the president. His sweat was acrid. Was that the smell of fear? Or of lying.

Maybe he wasn't lying when he said he was there, when Gold died. I wondered if anybody else was.

I went into the room and started toward Card, to whisper for him to get into the kitchen, but there was no need for secrecy. When everybody disappeared, the soldiers would figure it out, even if the president hadn't told them.

"We're gonna get out while the jet can still fly," I said in a loud voice.

"That's intelligent," one of the soldiers said laconically. "Leave us some ammo, please."

"You could bring the boxes up from downstairs," the other said.

"Got it." Dustin gestured for Card to follow him down.

"I should . . . I should stay and fight," Alba said.

The older soldier studied her black uniform. "You're just a cop, man. Save your skin." He smiled. "Thanks anyhow. And you're taking the vice president?"

"That's the idea."

He pursed his lips and nodded. I would've liked to have read his thoughts. "Boog, you hold down the fort here while I cover the escapees?"

"Gotcha. Try not to hit your commander in chief."

"No promises." He got up just as Boyer came through the door.

"Men," he started, "we've decided—"

"The Mars girl told us, sir," Duke said. "Gonna fly out of the rain." He looked at me. "Know where you're headed?"

"California, I think. A farm up in the north, where one of us grew up."

"Good luck. Finding anyplace safe."

"Good luck to you, too. Maybe if they know the president, the vice president, isn't here?"

"Acting president," Boyer said. "If only I were a better actor."

"We'll let them know," the other said. "No reason for them to believe us, though. And they'd still want Camp David and all the stuff here." A good reason to conspicuously leave, I thought. That would probably occur to them.

Would that constitute quitting one's post before being properly relieved? Does the principle still apply if your commander in chief deserts first?

The boys brought up the metal boxes and left them under the windows. We said good-bye to the soldiers and went out into the rain, following Paul and the president.

On the other side of the tarmac runway, there was a small control shack with radar and satellite dishes. Two men in blue flight suits stood on the porch, watching. The pilots of the two jets, probably. They waved casually, and I waved back. Would they fly after us? Probably not.

Or maybe they didn't want to hang around Camp David, either.

As we approached the NASA jet, a strip of fuselage swung down, becoming a staircase. No wide Martians to worry about.

The others hurried up the steps. Paul put a hand on Boyer's shoulder. "Wait."

"What for?"

"Just wait." I stepped slowly past them as the president shook loose. "You can't—"

"I think I can. This is my plane, and you're not getting on it."

"Don't you dare. I can have you shot down."

Paul looked at the assault rifle in his hands, and smiled. "Shall I pretend you didn't say that?" He gestured for me to go up the steps and then he followed me, backwards, keeping his eye on Boyer.

"You think they won't obey me."

"Pretty sure they won't. Go back and ask them."

He looked around, back up to the lodge, then the control shack. The two pilots stared back.

Then he started walking. "I'm going to stand right behind your exhaust. If you start the jet, you'll be a murderer."

Paul stepped inside and slapped a red button by the door, and turned to look down on the president. "You do what you will," he said as the stairs rose off the ground. "This thing doesn't have a rear view mirror."

I sat down and buckled up. "Is that true?"

He sat in the pilot seat and the harness clamped itself around him. "Well, sure. Where would you put a mirror?" A flatscreen blinked on and showed the black tarmac behind him.

The president stepped into view and planted his feet wide apart, standing with his hands on his hips.

"All this and stupid, too." He tapped a sequence of keys.

"You're going to—"

"Relax. The nozzle's more than a meter above his head. I could roast him if I goosed it, but I'll just bleed in a little fuel and creep away." He put on a headset. "Control, this is NASA 1." He paused. "Roger. We had to leave one behind for weight limitations. Taking off due north, into the wind? When we're over the clouds I'll take a heading of about 250°, destination Northern California." He nodded. "Roger, thanks. Same to you guys. Over and out."

The engine started with a loud pop, and I saw Boyer take off running. With a low whine, the plane inched forward.

"Everybody stay buckled in till I finish turning left above the weather. Then the flight attendant will come around with drinks." He laughed. "Oh, hell. We left him behind."

# 8

Nobody had said anything about drawing fire as we took off. I supposed whatever was going to happen would happen. Paul kept the plane low, treetop level, a minute or so after take-off, so I guess a person on the ground, with forest overhead, probably wouldn't have time to aim at us and fire.

Then I was pressed back into the seat and the plane roared and rattled as it screamed for altitude. We suddenly broke out of the clouds into afternoon sun but kept accelerating, almost straight up. After a minute, he throttled down and leveled off, green rounded mountaintops drifting by underneath us, sticking out of the misty clouds.

The cabin became quiet. Paul turned around in his seat and spoke normally. "Sorry; should've warned you. I wanted to get out of range, in case they had heat-seekers." He checked his watch.

"It'll take us about four hours to get to California. Landing sometime after three, Pacific time."

"Want to fly over Fruit Farm on the way?" Dustin said.

"Yeah, see if anybody's home."

"See if we draw any small-arms fire," Namir said. "That would help with our planning."

I reclined and closed my eyes, but there was no way I could sleep. Too much adrenaline, and whatever chemical follows it. I'd be nervous even if I didn't have anything to be nervous about.

Card and Alba and Dustin had rearranged the rear of the plane so it had seats around a table. Card had found a notebook made of sheets of paper. Each page had the presidential seal and Mervyn Gold's name embossed (in gold) at the top. He was drawing a complicated geometrical doodle with a pencil, filling the page from the upper left-hand corner down. It was actually beautiful, in a rigid formal way.

I sat down next to him. "I didn't know you had artistic talent."

"I don't; this 'me' doesn't. Picked up some from my second avatar."

Dustin looked up from his book. "Your different personae had different skill sets?"

"Yeah. Pity we don't have the third one here. He was the negotiator, the businessman."

"You learned from both of them?" I asked.

"It's not like learning." He shrugged. "Sort of 'being,' actually. There's a quantum-chemistry explanation; they start out as perfect duplicates, but begin to diverge in a microsecond or so. Personality more than specific skills. You would have liked either of them more than the original."

I squeezed his arm. "You'll do."

"The other two," Dustin said, "did they have separate social lives? Different circles of friends?"

"Yes and no . . . we overlapped, and everyone we knew was aware that there were three of me. It's not really complicated. Most of my friends have at least one avatar."

"Feel lonely now?" Alba asked.

"Yeah. You never doubled?"

"Couldn't afford it. Actually, it was pretty low on the list of stuff I wanted."

He nodded. "Well, when you get older . . . if it's ever possible again."

He was starting to tremble. I stroked his arm and his smooth head when he faced me. "You got a sister back, anyhow."

"A younger sister." He smiled. "That's stranger than my dupes."

After a pause, Alba said, "Any way you can get them back?"

He grimaced. "Yes and no. The physical bodies are just . . . spoiled meat. Some version of their personalities ought to be hard-filed somewhere. Ought to be. I could sue if they're not."

"Carmen, you want to get me a bite?" Paul called back. "Better not leave the stick." The autopilot would take us straight to Fruit Farm unless the power went out. Then it would be nice to have someone up there who knew how and where to point the plane.

I rummaged through the bag of stuff from the NASA vending machine and got him a cookie and some nuts, and a bottle of water. He gave me a peck on the cheek when I delivered the snacks.

There were two auxiliary screens on, one with some porn thing and the other with page 13 of *Pride and Prejudice*. He probably wanted me to comment, but I wouldn't.

The top part of the windshield was darkened to blot out the sun. It was solid clouds underneath, as far as I could see. "I wonder how far the clouds go."

"No telling. Feels funny, not having the weather." His voice dropped. "How is your brother doing?"

"Hard to say. Trying to sort things out, I suppose."

"He may be more help than Dustin, dealing with the commune."

"Maybe. I'll talk to them."

"Ply him with peanuts," he said, crunching down on a mouthful.

Maybe a near beer. I picked up a couple and put them on the table and sat down.

"Thanks. Are we on course?"

"Headed west, anyhow." I watched him pop the can and take a drink. "What do you think these communists will be like?"

"Communists? Like people in the commune?"

"What would you call them, then?"

"Earthers. Most of them. Not sure what they call themselves."

"You've never been up there?"

"God, no. It's at the other end of the state. Long way to go for fresh vegetables. Wish I had, now."

"Yeah; we don't really know what to expect."

Dustin put down his book. "Quietly crazy. That's what I expect. Who knows, though, after seventy years."

"Noisy and crazy," Card said. "Trigger-happy hillbillies. That's a cube cliché."

That was interesting. "With a basis in fact?"

"Not Fruit Farm specifically. Back around the turn of the century, 2100, some communes in the East got together and raised some hell. They tried to secede from the United States, piecemeal. They were followers of that guy . . ."

"Lazlo Motkin," Alba said.

"Yeah. They had a regular little war."

"They weren't even one geographical area," Alba said. "Spread out over three or four states. They claimed there was an 'existential border' between them and us."

"They had lawyers to prove it?"

"Lawyers and guns," Card said. "What more do you need?"

"Anything come of it?" I asked.

Card shook his head. "All over in a couple of months. Some people jailed, some leaders executed. Lazlo Motkin himself died in a military action."

"Which was embarrassing to America," Alba said. "He was running for president at the time. He was just a rich crackpot until he died. Then he became a symbol of government oppression."

I had a vague memory of him sending us a loony message on the starship. If we were good Americans, we would do a kamikaze strike on the Others' home world.

"We ought to start out assuming they are nice rational people," Elza said, "who have some nineteenth-century ideas about things like electricity."

"Wonder if they'll have power after Wednesday," Alba said. "The only people in the whole country?"

"Not if the Others do the same thing as before," Dustin said. "Everything stopped working, even batteries. Stuff like hydroelectric power and wind machines. Kept turning around, but without making any juice.

"The question is whether living with this archaic technology makes the Fruit Farmers better equipped for dealing with the brave new world that's coming. We're assuming so, but you can argue that their technological primitivism is only skin-deep. They've had electricity all along—home-made, but what's the difference?"

Namir had gone to the head in back of the plane, and he emerged with a bottle of whisky and a stack of cups. "Let's drink to NASA and their legendary foresight."

I had a small glass of the stuff, smoky and smooth, and before I finished it, a curtain of fatigue fell over me like a sedative. I walked unsteadily back to my seat, reclined it, and was asleep before my head hit the plastic pillow.

# 9

I woke suddenly when the plane's engine throttled down, and we banked sharply. I raised the curtain on my window and saw that we were angling down over some heavily forested hilly land. There was a small, meandering river.

"Should be only a few miles," Paul said, his amplified voice flat and crackling. "I'm going down low and dead slow, and will cut the engine as we glide over the commune. Your flatscreens should be showing what's directly under us." I reached forward and tapped the screen on the back of the seat in front of me. Treetops rolled by underneath, slowly growing larger as we dropped.

They must hear us coming. Were people running for cover? Running to man the anti-aircraft lasers?

"They won't have lasers." Namir was reading my mind. "A shotgun could do some damage, though."

"Why no lasers?"

"They could. But they aren't getting megawatts out of twentieth-century solar cells and wind machines."

The forest abruptly stopped, replaced by squares of pasture and fruit trees in neat lines. We were low enough that I could see cows looking up at us. The engine stuttered off, and we glided with a sound of rushing air.

A stockade wall and a glimpse of blue rectangle—a swimming pool where a half dozen naked people pointed at us. Two of them waved, much better than pointing guns.

Just past the pool was a large low building. "That's the common," Dustin said. "We used to go there to watch cube." Past that were dozens of individual dwellings, I supposed multi-family. It looked as if they all started out with a basic octagonal shape, and grew in various directions.

People with clothes on looked up at us, shading their eyes from the low sun. At the entrance to the stockade, a man had a small assault rifle on a sling hanging from his shoulder. He watched us go over without raising the gun.

There were watchtowers at each corner of the stockade. From our angle you couldn't see who or what was in them. There was a shed at the entrance to the place, probably where they sold to outsiders. Then a dirt road that cut through more pasture and fruit trees, before it plunged into the forest.

Paul turned the engine back on with a pop and a quiet roar, and we gained a little altitude. "Now let's see how far we'll have to walk," he said.

We followed the winding river for a couple of minutes. A dirt path went alongside it, maybe adequate for a jepé, but not wide or straight enough for landing. Then the gray strip of an autoway slid by. Paul rose up in a banking curl, crossing over the river and then back again. He lined up perfectly with the middle lane, and eased the plane down. No sign of any auto traffic, but this probably wasn't a busy road even under normal conditions.

The brakes chirped a couple of times, and we rolled to a halt just over the river, taking up all of the right-hand lane.

"Namir, you spies could earn your keep here. Take a look around?"

"Got it." He and Dustin and Elza took weapons and bandoliers from the overhead compartments as the door swung down to become stairs. I was eager to get some fresh air myself, but Paul was right. Send the guns out first. The bridge might be guarded, or at least watched.

"I wonder how safe we are," Card said. "If a car comes, it should brake automatically, but . . ."

"Trust to our luck," I said. "So far so good."

"That makes me feel so safe."

"You probably couldn't get onto the autoway if the failsafes weren't working," Alba said. "The power shuts down automatically."

"Government intrusion," he said. "Any zero can hotwire a car into manual."

"Can you?" I asked.

He shrugged. "I know how." Yeah, like I know how a starship works.

Namir and Elza were pointing their guns up and down the road, while Dustin jogged to the side of the bridge. He looked over and then signaled with a shrug.

Namir came back up the steps. "I suggest Plan P," he said. "We probably can't make it to the farm before dark."

"Excuse me?" I said. "Did I sleep through something?"

"P stands for prudence," Namir said. "The plane is too conspicuous a target to stay in. So we unload the essentials and hide nearby."

"Like on the road here."

"No, we'll carry stuff back into the woods." He looked at Paul. "Maybe down by the river?"

"Have to carry it down sooner or later."

I slung a rifle cross-ways over my back and collected a couple of bags of food and stuff. When Dustin came aboard, I asked him whether the river water would be safe to drink. He counseled caution until we could ask a native. "I drank from it as a kid, but Dad gave me hell."

After several minutes of no traffic, Card and Alba agreed that the autoway must be turned off. That doesn't mean someone couldn't come screaming along on manual, but we could hear them coming and get off the roadway.

There was no actual path from the bridge down to the dirt road along the river. We picked our way down slippery gravel and through a thicket of brambles, the spies preceding us with their guns. After we got to solid ground, they left us with most of the artillery and went up for another load.

It was peaceful and pretty. The river was about ten meters wide, swift, and looked deep.

Card came and stood beside me, looking into the water. "Remember the Galápagos?"

"Sure." We'd had a day there before we left for Mars on the space elevator. "You ever go back?"

"I did about twenty years ago. Diving and fishing."

"You became a sportsman?"

"Kind of. Took a motorsled to the North Pole once; that was interesting."

"Living off polar bears and penguins?"

"No penguins there. Mostly beers and hot dogs. I did see a polar bear, but it ran away."

"Never went back to Mars?"

"Never really wanted to. Got out as soon as the quarantine lifted. So glad to get back here." He took a drink of water from a plastic bottle and offered it to me. I took a drink even though I wasn't thirsty.

"That's Mars," he said.

"I guess." Impolite to refuse water.

"You liked it there."

"It's home. Became home." I shook my head. "Was home. Never going back."

"No one ever can. If you want to be philosophical."

"Ever go back to Florida?"

"Yeah. The old house was still there, but with big condos all around it. One quaint old cottage with the rose bushes still there. Same pink gravel lawn. Surrounded by sky-highs."

"That's funny."

"What?"

"Must've been some zoning peculiarity."

He laughed. "Carmen . . . it's a fucking *museum*. It's the last place on Earth where the Mars Girl lived."

"Oh, shit."

"You ought to go. Maybe they'd let you in for free."

"I could wear my authentic Martian cuntsuit." What adults called a skinsuit.

"In Florida? You'd be arrested."

"They don't seem too inhibited here. You see the people around the pool?"

"Yeah, California. Love it."

Dustin and Elza were struggling down the slope with the NASA mail cart. We went up to help them through the brush.

"Paul's making a list," Elza said. "What we can leave on the plane."

"Does it lock up?" Card asked.

"He says yes. But you could get in with a can opener."

"Probably smart to take all the weapons and ammunition," Elza said.

"Assuming the nice folks at Fruit Farm will feed us," I said.

"If they don't, we'll be on our own in a couple of days anyhow," Elza said unnecessarily.

Namir came out of the woods, kicking aside brambles. "Found a place where we can spend tonight."

"A motel?" My brother said.

Namir ignored him. "Small clearing with plenty of overhead cover."

"In case the prez sends his space force?" Elza said.

"Could happen. Or the folks at Fruit Farm might come down the road looking for us."

"Armed with pitchforks and trowels," Dustin said.

"They have weapons. We should be ready for anything."

Of course. I gestured to Alba. "Let's go up and get a load."

We picked our way up and found that Paul had made a neat stack of stuff beside the plane.

I picked up one of the three laser rifles, I think the one I'd had at Camp David. Not much charge.

Paul came down the steps and answered my question before I could ask it. "It'll be useless junk after Wednesday, but I didn't want to leave them behind. Somebody could get them tonight or tomorrow and use them on us."

"This one's almost dry."

"Still a potent psychological weapon, till Wednesday." He set down the two bags he was carrying, food and the flare guns from the motor pool. "Or you could throw it in the river. Two's probably enough." We also had the powder weapons from Alba's trunk, and the ones Namir had "found."

"Take out the fuel cell before you throw it away," Alba said. "I'll carry it till Wednesday." I extracted it and gave it to her, then tossed the thing spinning over the side. It hit the water with a quiet splash, bobbed up once, and sank.

Paul was balancing a flare pistol in his hand. "I could torch the plane," he said. "Burn our bridges literally." He shook his head. "We might need it if the farm doesn't work out. Go find that island."

"Native girls with bare boobs," I said. "You have them here."

We went down to Namir's clearing and made a laughable kind of campsite out of it. If it rained, we would just have to get wet. But we got enough pine boughs to make a couple of large beds. Needed only be sleeping five at a time, two on guard.

It was getting cool as the sun went down, but we decided against making a fire.

I was on the first guard shift, seven till nine, hiding in some bushes between the road and the river. Sipped cold instant coffee and listened for anything that wasn't water and wind. I had a laser rifle and one of the flare pistols. Elza had the same armament, hiding in the woods north of our camp. If we saw or heard something, we were supposed to close our eyes, to preserve dark vision, and shoot a flare straight up. Perhaps starting a forest fire.

At first I felt all crawly, but convinced myself it wasn't bugs. Just skin crud. Dried sweat from crossing ten or twelve time zones. Maybe we could take a dip in the river before we left.

I thought about Snowbird and hoped she was happy and healing. Maybe they'd chip a hole in the ice so she could go swimming.

It was a cloudless night and so not completely dark, with the moonglow. My heart gave a jump when I distinctly heard steps, a quiet crunch and slide of gravel at the end of the overpass, but it was just a small deer, coming over to see what was on the other side. Fascinating to watch it picking its way down, cautious but not careful enough. If I'd been a hunter, she would've been venison.

I could smell her, a funny, musky odor. Which meant she couldn't smell me, I suppose, the wind coming this way. All of my experience with animals was before I had turned nineteen. That deer was more exotic than a Martian.

Less strange than the Other that we glimpsed, though. My skin crawled a different way, remembering the chitinous monstrosity. Our absentee masters now. As slow and inexorable as the wheeling stars.

The stars were bright here. Bright everywhere, after Wednesday. I wondered whether Wolf 25, the Others' home, was visible. It was pretty dim, twenty-five light-years away. Paul said it was in the constellation Pisces. That wasn't one of the five or six I knew.

I'd spent years barreling through interstellar space, out among the lonely stars, but didn't spend much time looking at them. No windows to stare out of.

Mars was unmistakable, a bright, orange, unblinking star. Why did they call it the Red Planet? Didn't the ancients have a word for orange? Maybe red was more dramatic.

The deer caught a whiff of something and bounded away through the woods, its white tail a dim bouncing flag. Don't shoot, Elza. She didn't.

Paul's watch glowed with old-fashioned hands and numerals, temporarily useful. I didn't look at it for what I estimated to be an hour, which turned out to be thirty-two minutes.

I tried to concentrate on sights and sounds, almost unchanging. Every few minutes a bird would tweet or hoot. I watched a bright star crawl through the trees. It's a good thing I wasn't sleepy. Even so, I kept falling into a meditative state, perhaps encouraged by the rushing water.

The way smells changed was interesting. Subtle but sudden, as the breeze shifted, and some new blossom or bush dominated momentarily. I guess it happens in the city, too, but we're too overloaded with stimuli to notice.

It occurred to me that we were downstream from the farm. If they knew or suspected we were near the overpass, they could float down silently on canoes or rafts. I gazed at the river for a bit, but realized that approaching us that way would be really conspicuous, even at night. A small stick floating along was easy to see, disrupting the moonglow's reflection. So I went back to where I'd been, and sat down quietly between two low bushes.

My quietness was rewarded with another animal visitation, a masked raccoon that came down the same path the deer had used, but making no noise. When it got to the road, it beetled off the other way, investigating the darkness under the overpass. Maybe I should be hiding there. Along with the bugs and snakes, no thanks. The raccoon was probably after a meal, one that I wouldn't find appealing.

Sooner than I'd expected, Card came across to relieve me. His white tropical tourist outfit made him a conspicuous ghost, moving in the moonglow. In another couple of weeks, the tunic would be dirty enough to use as camouflage.

"Anything?" he whispered.

"Two animals, a deer and a raccoon." I passed him Paul's watch and the rifle and flare pistol. "You know what to do with this?"

"Straight up, eyes closed."

"You won't have any trouble staying awake?"

"No. Haven't slept yet."

"Keep an eye on the river."

"Yeah. They could have a navy."

It was darker in the forest than I'd expected. I walked carefully, slowly picking my way uphill. If I came to the autoway, I'd missed them. I almost stepped on Paul, his NASA jumpsuit a deeper black against the shadow. Then someone started to snore a few yards away, I couldn't tell who.

I knelt and patted the bed of pine boughs next to him, then crawled in not quite close enough to touch. I could smell his hair, though, along with the pine, and could hear his soft breath.

What a long day, quartering the planet and coming to ground in this dark wood. I closed my eyes and slept like a tired child.

# 10

After an energy-bar breakfast and cold coffee, we carried all our stuff down to the road and started walking, Namir in front and Dustin bringing up the rear, each of them armed with laser and pistol. It was a little too military for me, bad first impression, but I kept it to myself. We might be walking into an ambush.

The plane had measured a straight-line distance of 7.4 miles from the commune to the highway. That would probably come to about ten miles along the winding river road. So we should reach the commune by mid-day. My feet were a little tired and perhaps blistered. I felt every pebble in the road through my thin-soled shoes, but could avoid the big and sharp ones.

When we first started walking, we startled a deer drinking at the river's edge. From then on the animals stayed away from us.

Better woodsmen might have suspected that the lack of wildlife meant that we weren't alone. But our military contingent mainly knew the perils presented by city and desert. Namir did study the trees for snipers, I noticed, and scanned the ground, I supposed for trip wires and mines.

The semi-wild sylvan setting had been preserved, back in Dustin's time here, by government edict. Thousands of acres had been gathered up and added to an existing federal parkland. Fruit Farm was "grandfathered in," allowed to stay and operate as a private, non-mechanized cultural relic. We walked by what remained of the old mechanized farms, doomed by unprofitability to return to nature. Abandoned machinery turned into elaborate birdhouses, streaked with rust and guano. The vegetation that had replaced pasture and farmland, mostly scrub pine, was not as heavy and shadowy as the older forests, and it felt safer walking alongside it.

After about an hour and a half, we stopped under the shade of an old oak to rest, breaking out sandwiches from the NASA vending machines, welcome but starting to go a little stale.

Paul sorted through the stuff in the rolling mailbag. "We have food for two or three days, if they turn us away. What if we have to go back to the plane and find that it's been vandalized—or just gone?"

"You said not many people could fly it," Card said.

"Land it. It wouldn't take much skill to take off, and then crash somewhere. I'm just wondering whether it might be towed away by some highway maintenance machine. Or pushed into the river to keep the road clear."

"I'd guess not," Card said. "I don't think the maintenance robots are going anywhere without satellite communication and GPS."

"Let's worry about that when we have to," Namir said. "How do we approach the commune? They'll probably be expecting us."

"They might be having lots of visitors," Dustin said. "It's going to be a popular place, once the power goes off permanently."

"Sure," Card said. "That accounts for the traffic jam all around us." A butterfly wafted by in the quiet air. "This place would be in the middle of nowhere even if the autoway was working. You can't just pull off the autoway and start hiking. People without airplanes would have to start wherever this road starts. And it's probably not on maps."

"Didn't used to be," Dustin said. "People who wanted our produce would make a day of it. Drive up this dusty old road with no signs."

"Must've been pretty good vegetables," I said.

"People are funny. We'd sell them stuff like elephant garlic, that we'd buy in bulk down in Sacramento. If it was odd, they would assume we grew it here."

"Looked like a lot of crops when we flew over."

"Bigger than when I was a kid, and we were more than self-sufficient then."

"You said there were a couple of hundred back then," I said. "Doesn't look like that many now."

"Hard to say, the hour we flew over. Lot of people resting up after morning chores and lunch."

Namir sat down at the base of the oak and studied the scene with binoculars. He braced his elbow on his knee and turned the zoom lever all the way up, looking back down the road.

"See anything?" Elza said.

He shook his head slightly, still staring. "Feels like we're being followed."

"I had that feeling, too," I said. "I thought it was just nerves."

"Probably." He lowered the binoculars, rubbed his eyes, and raised them to look again. Sharp intake of breath. "There." His voice dropped to a whisper. "Sun glint off something. Maybe metal, maybe a lens. Maybe a shiny leaf."

"Sniper?" Paul said.

"No. I don't think so. A rifle scope would be hooded, sniper or hunter. There it is again."

I carefully didn't look in that direction. "What should we do?"

"I'm tempted to wave and see if they wave back. If it's a sniper with a gig laser, we're all pot roast anyhow."

"Like someone would carry that much weight into the woods," Dustin said. "Even if the Earthers had one."

Namir set down the binoculars and leaned back against the tree. He folded his hands on his chest and closed his eyes. "Probably wouldn't be your Earthers, anyhow. More likely someone like us, interlopers after all that good organic food."

Something splashed in the river, and I jumped. "Should we do something?"

"Just relax. We'll be back in the woods in a couple hundred meters. I'll hide at the edge and see if anyone's following us."

"We'll be at the farm in another hour and a half," Paul said.

"I'll catch up. Leave one of the cells with me."

I handed him mine. "Punch number one for Paul."

He smiled at Paul. "Does this mean we're a couple now?"

"Oral only. I have standards."

"Two condoms." He put the phone in his shirt pocket. "I'll call before I leave. Or if I see anything."

We rested under the tree for a while and then walked on unhurriedly. When we came to the woods where the river curved, Namir silently stepped into the brush and disappeared.

Dustin walked past me to take Namir's point position and looked toward where he'd gone. "I'm impressed," he said sotto voce.

I wasn't sure this was smart. Namir was the only one of us who actually *looked* dangerous. That might be important in a confrontation.

Paul and I were as recognizable as movie stars, and to a lot of people we were symbols of treason. Cooperating with the Martians, giving in to the Others. Dustin looked like a college kid and Elza, a fashion model. Alba was so small she looked like a girl wearing a cop costume, though the riot gun gave her a certain air of authority. Card looked like an overweight couch vegetable, which I guess he was.

Namir had something in his eyes that the rest of us lacked. Not arrogance, but a kind of physical confidence, certainty. Like he'd done everything, and most of it well. He'd told me, though, back at the motor pool last night, that Card was the kind of guy you'd watch out for in a bar fight. Heavy but not slow, and hard to knock down.

Of course, you could always go to a different class of bar.

I was always kind of curious about that aspect of Earth culture, American culture. I'd left before I was old enough to drink legally, most places, so my experience was limited to one beer joint in the

Galápagos, the Orbit Hilton, and the dome in Mars. On Mars, actually, above the colony. No boisterous drunks anywhere, no fisticuffs, just the occasional voice raised in dispute over a Scrabble word. All the fun I'd missed. But I did know not to pick a fight with someone who looked like my brother.

I'd forgotten how good it was to be out walking—my *body* had forgotten. Dutifully treading on the treadmill on *ad Astra*, walking one day and jogging the next, was no substitute for the real thing, no matter how exact or exotic the VR surround was. Walking the Malibu beach or the skyways of Koala Lumpur, my body knew I was a hamster on a treadmill in an interstellar cage.

I walked along like that, in a reverie, for maybe an hour, everybody not talking and not bunching up. We were trying to be inconspicuous but not sneaky, in case someone was watching or trailing us.

Then a familiar sound, the toy-piano Mozart Paul used on his cell. He put it to his ear and whispered something, then gave it a shake and tried again.

"Could it be low?" I said.

"I don't know. It got a flash charge at the motor pool. Should still be good."

He shrugged and held it out to me. The ON button glowed green. I put it to my ear. "Namir? Hello?" Nothing but a white-noise sound.

"Could he have turned yours on accidentally?"

"Don't see how." I handed his back. "I mean, you might turn it on, but you wouldn't punch up the number accidentally."

"Give it to me," Elza said. "Hush." She listened to it, stopping her other ear. After a minute she shook her head and handed it back. "If it's in his pocket, you ought to hear something when he moves."

"Unless he's not moving," I said.

We all flinched at a sudden machine-gun sound. "Just a woodpecker," Alba said. "Pileated." It was a big thing, right over us, bright red head.

I held up the phone. "So should I just talk to him?"

Elza nodded, still staring at the bird. "Yeah. Tell him to turn it off."

"Hello, Namir?" I repeated his name twice, louder. "Maybe he turned it on accidentally, and dropped it?"

"Or there's something wrong with it," Paul said. "So we either go back and check on him, or wait for him here, or move on."

"Move on," Elza said when he looked at her. Everybody seemed to agree, except perhaps me. That cell phone had done some screwy things, but I didn't remember it making calls on its own.

A couple more curves in the river, and we were almost there. The stockade looked more formidable from the ground than it had from the plane.

We studied it from hiding, on the edge of the woods, over a long, empty parking lot. To the right and left were cornfields, regularly spaced plants two and three feet high. The produce stand was empty, with a hand-lettered sign saying ARMAGEDDON OUT OF BUSINESS SALE. No guards visible, but the two guard towers probably had people behind the dark aiming slots.

The road had a chain across it with a CLOSED sign. "We ought to just leave the weapons behind and walk up to the door," Paul said.

"I don't know," Dustin said. "No ace in the hole? We should leave someone in reserve."

"How about just the women?" Elza said. "Carmen and Alba and I walk up to them unarmed. Buck naked."

"No way," Alba said.

"In underwear?" She grinned.

"I don't have underwear, and you know it," I said. "Let's go back to 'no guns.'"

"I *am* naked without a gun," Alba said. "But it makes sense." She took off her cop jacket and I left behind the sweater I'd stolen from Camp David, under which I might have concealed something more dangerous than my natural endowments. Elza left behind the pistol she'd been carrying in her waistband, the one that Paul had killed with. Protecting me.

Alba checked her cell and it worked on Paul's number. She left the phone turned on and we set off, trying to walk casually despite being stared at, presumably from both sides.

It was still a dirt road, but hard like asphalt. I asked Alba about it.

"It's probably laser-fused," she said. "A lot of country folks do driveways like that."

"Nice to know they have big lasers," Elza said.

"Might have been hired out."

"Stop right there," an amplified male voice said. "Put up your hands."

We were only about halfway to the door, maybe fifty meters away. It opened slightly, and two people came out in thick body armor with assault rifles. One of them beckoned.

We kept our hands raised and walked toward them. They didn't point guns at us, but kept them ready, what the boys called "port arms."

"You're from the plane," one of them said, a man.

"That's right," Elza said.

"Where are the others?"

"God damn," the other one said, a woman. "You're the Mars Girl."

"When I was a girl," I said automatically.

"How many others, Mars Girl?" the man said. "You can put your hands down."

"Four." We hadn't discussed whether to lie.

"Hiding in the woods? Watching us?" He was looking past me, at the tree line.

"That's right."

"I think you mean three."

"We got the one you left back down the road," the woman said.

"You *got* him? What did you do?"

"Come inside," the man said. He tipped his weapon toward the door.

"He's my husband," Elza said. "What did you do to him?"

"Inside."

We went through the door and found ourselves surrounded by forty or fifty staring people in a crowded semicircle. There were some children and even two babes in arms. Two dogs, no guns. More women than men.

"Is this all of you?" I said.

"You don't need to know," the man said, but a couple of people shook their heads no. Somebody whispered the "the Mars Girl." The burden of fame.

A big white man, bald with a close-cropped gray beard, stepped forward. He looked at the armed and armored man. His voice was loud and harsh: "Where are the others?"

"Hiding back in the woods."

"Still heavily armed, I assume." He pointed at the cell on Alba's belt. "You want to call them and tell them to come on in? Unarmed, like you."

"No, sir. I can't do that."

" 'Sir,' is it?" He reached to the small of his back and drew a small black pistol. He put his other hand out. "Give me the phone."

She did, and he looked at the green light, nodded, and spoke into it: "You've got five minutes. Come on in without your weapons, or I'll shoot the black woman. Five minutes more, I shoot the black-haired one. Five minutes after that, the Mars Girl goes to heaven." He pointed the gun up and fired it, a loud bang that echoed off the walls, and looked at his watch. He turned off the phone and handed it back to Alba.

"You're serious," she said.

"Oh, we're always serious, here at Funny Farm."

"I thought you were Fruit Farm," I said.

"That was a joke, back when 'fruit' meant homosexual. It's not funny anymore."

"We meant to join you," I said, "but if we're not welcome, we can go on our way."

"We'll talk about that." Alba's phone beeped. "You can answer that."

She did. "Hello . . . yes, he has." She held up the phone. "He wants to talk to you."

"Your leader?" Alba shrugged. "If he wants to talk, he has to come here. He has four minutes and ten seconds." He looked at his watch. "You have. Four minutes five seconds."

"We have weapons," Elza said, "but we never intended to use them on you. Only to add to the farm's defenses." Her voice was harsh and strained. Could he see that she was tensed to attack?

He stared at her. "What do you think they'll do?"

"Why don't *you* think, for a change, Rico?" A gray-haired woman walked out of the crowd. "This is not the way."

She stood next to him with her hands on her hips. "I have a good idea. Let's have the farm surrounded with a group of armed men, and then threaten to kill their women. Maybe they'll leave their guns outside and come in for a chat." She stepped closer to him. "Or maybe they'll think with their balls, like some people I know, and come over the walls shooting, with nothing to lose."

"I wasn't really going to—"

"I know that, but what do *they* know?" She held out her hand to Alba. "Let me talk to them, quick."

She took the phone. "Hello, hello? That ay-hole who just talked to you is not our leader."

"Look, Roz—" She shot him a silencing look.

"Your people are free to leave," she said into the cell, "and I wouldn't blame them if they did. Or you could come join them, and we could talk." She listened for a moment, nodding. "Okay. Which one of you is Carmen?"

I held out my hand, and she gave me the phone. It was Paul. "If it's safe for us to come in, tell me where we first met."

"Galápagos," I said. "But wait." I looked at the man with the gun. "What did you do to the man we left behind?"

"A tranquilizer dart. He's still sleeping."

"We want to see him, before this goes any further."

"Easy enough," the woman said. I followed her to the nearest building, which had a silver letter A over the door.

Namir was lying on a cot under a window, his shirt off and a white bandage around his neck. I felt above the bandage for a pulse. It was regular but shallow. "How did you get him past us?"

"GEV," she said, ground-effect vehicle. "We took him around you, along the autoway."

I asked Paul whether he'd gotten all that, and he had. "We'll leave Card behind with most of the stuff."

Roz and I went back outside. "So he's not the leader. Are you?"

She laughed. "No one is, technically. It's a paradise of democratic anarchy. But I was elected Primus this year, 'first among equals.' I get to listen to everybody and suggest who's wrong."

"Do you have any friends left?"

"A few. Life became simpler here when the whole world decided to join us in anarchy. We just chased all the strangers off and blew down two bridges. People can get to us, but it's not easy."

"That's why there wasn't anybody on the highway, the autoway?"

"Right. Takes a plane, and who knows how to fly one without satellites? You guys surprised us."

"Glad you didn't shoot us down."

"Two people asked for permission. By the time I could respond, you were gone."

"What would you have said?"

"Bring me their heads and save the bodies for the stewpot." She smiled. "It was pretty obvious where you'd be landing. There was a lookout party in the woods with the GEV, so I called them and had them go take a look."

"You're pretty well-equipped for a bunch of Earthers."

"Well, some of us are practical. But it's back to nature for everybody Wednesday, right?"

"That's what the Others say. Not like they've never lied."

"Wait, now . . . the Mars Girl? You've actually met the Others?"

"Yes and no. They were behind glass, two-hundred-some degrees below zero. They talked to us through their intermediary, Spy, but it was like a pre-recorded message. Always is."

"On the cube they look like big lobsters."

"Kind of." A lobster is a close cousin in comparison.

"Must've been terrifying."

"We were scared." But in a sense we weren't, not in any familiar way. Helpless and in mortal danger, but it was so unreal that normal emotions were suspended, confused. I remembered smelling peanuts on Paul's breath and wondering what the aliens would smell like, if we could smell them, but there was nothing else in the frosty air, just peanuts.

*How can you tell when you're kissing an elephant?* went the joke when I was a girl. *You can smell the peanuts on his breath.*

"Do you have cube here, in case they send another message?" Elza said.

She nodded. "Somebody's watching all the time. Fucking depressing, twenty-four-hour news. But nothing's new."

A young man walked over from the group at the door. "Two of them on their way, Roz." We followed him back.

Paul and Dustin were carrying laser rifles. When they were about twenty feet away, they set them on the ground, and warily continued.

I stepped into the doorway, and Paul rushed to me. "You all right?"

"Fine. Namir seems okay, just sedated."

"Police-issue tranquilizer dart," Roz said from behind me, and held out her hand. "Oralee Roswell. They call me Roz."

He looked through the door at all the people, nodding, counting. "So I guess it's your move, Roz. What do we do now?"

She squinted up at the sun. "Too early for dinner. Come in for a drink?" The big gray-bearded guy, Rico, watched this exchange with a blank expression. He came along when we followed her, though.

The dining hall was a few decades past its prime, fading peeling green paint on warped plywood walls. It reminded me of the way the cafeteria smelled when I was a little girl. Layers of old stale food. We went through the dining hall, though, to a screened-in porch with clean blue plastic furniture and a nice rich farm smell from the pastures that surrounded it.

We made introductions on the way. It turned out that Dustin's story was familiar to them; people at the Farm had been following our fortunes since we left the earth. The fact that his parents had left Fruit Farm as dissenting rebels had been forgotten. He was the Farm's only famous alumnus.

Two other elders joined us, pulling together two of the plastic tables. One, probably male, was wraithlike, pale, tall, and thin, with a wispy halo of white hair.

"This building was new when we left," Dustin said. "We kids helped paint the outside. It was dark red then, like a barn."

"I remember it being red," Rico said thoughtfully. "They painted it white when I was about ten."

"Green after you left Earth," the pale one said. "In the nineties sometime. Thanks, Analese." A girl of about ten had brought in a tray of cups of steaming brown liquid with a mild aroma.

"We can't grow coffee or tea here, of course, so we get used to this stuff. Yerba Buena."

I tasted it. Maybe I wouldn't get used to it. "You said you blew down two bridges what, yesterday?"

"A few hours after the power went out. We had some early-morning customers we had to escort out, first."

"You just happened to have lots of high explosives lying around?" Dustin said, "And you knew how to use them?"

"We've been ready for a long time, since before I was born. The elders called it Code Red. It goes back to Lazlo's Rebellion, when a total breakdown outside seemed possible, probable."

"I was one of the bridge team," Rico said. "Four of us trained by elders, where to set the charges and what to do. They'd been trained by their elders, and so on."

"Lucky the charges still worked."

"Yes. The alternative directions seemed more wishful thinking than sound engineering. But the antique explosives worked fine."

"It was pretty loud even here," Roz said.

Namir appeared at the door, walking unsteadily, a young woman supporting his elbow.

"The sleeper wakes," Paul said.

"I walked right into a set-up," he said. "As soon as you were out of sight, they popped me with a dart."

"Our good luck and your bad," the woman said. "I tried to aim for your shoulder, but you moved too fast. Wouldn't hurt so much."

He patted her on the back in mock affection. "My assailant, Miche Onadato. Glad you missed my eyes."

I touched him. "You're feeling all right now?"

He smiled at me. "Better than all right. What was in that shot you just gave me?"

"Epinephrine. You'll feel great until you don't."

Roz brought over a chair for him. "So does your group have a plan?"

Dustin spoke first. "I guess our plan was to see whether you had a plan."

Roz shook her head slowly. "It's a farm. The calendar and the weather make our plans for us."

"We know a lot about agriculture," I said, "if you need help maintaining starship hydroponics."

"You can grow a lot on twenty square meters, if you don't have anything else to do," Dustin said.

"When I was young, I did a lot of dirt farming on the kibbutz," Namir said. "I could probably still control a shovel."

Rico was studying him. "I think we'd rather have you on patrol, for the time being. You have military experience?"

"Of a kind." Before he surrendered his commission, he was a colonel in the Mossad.

"Unlike us, he's been shot at," Dustin said. "Elza and I were intelligence officers, too, for the US. But I never shot at anything any more dangerous than a target."

"Me neither," Elza said, "until the other day."

"I heard about that on the news," Roz said. "You lost one of your number."

"Stray round." My voice caught. "She was just standing in the kitchen."

Roz shook her head. "Sorry."

"Probably be a lot of shooting," Rico said, "before everybody runs out of ammo. Not many of us gonna be dying of old age."

Roz gave him a tired look. "Maybe here."

"You've been watching the news," Elza said. "Is it all bad?"

Rico said yes, but Roz shook her head no. "There are other places like this, where they're self-sufficient and well defended. Eugene, Oregon, is the closest."

"You're in contact with them?" I asked.

"Just by cell. Till Wednesday. I talked to their town manager, Benjie what's-his-name?"

"Sweeney," Rico supplied.

"Benjamin Sweeney."

"We decided to have a meeting, a physical meeting, the first of every month. Starting a month from now, June first."

"What were you going to meet about?" Paul asked.

She shrugged. "First off, a damage appraisal. See what we have and how we might help each other."

"They have something you don't?"

"Books, mainly. Non-electronic, printed paper books. Tens of thousands of them."

"Why on Earth?" Elza said. "Is it a museum?"

"I guess it will be, and a library. Right now it's a huge antique bookstore. There was a cube special about it, a couple of weeks ago. When it was just a curiosity."

"Probably one in every big city," Rico said. "Burned to the ground by now. So Eugene's is special."

I remembered Dad taking us to a huge paper bookstore in St. Petersburg, when I was little. Rare even then, I did a report on it for school. The owner had died of a mosquito bite in Africa, I suppose looking for books.

"Thought we'd talk to them about trading," Roz said. "We have a lot of books, a couple of hundred. Not many of them useful, though."

"Long walk?" I asked.

"A week or so. Depending on how straight a route we take."

"You could fly," Paul said. "I could get you there in twenty minutes."

She cocked her head at him. "How big an operation would that be?"

"If the plane hasn't been damaged, just have to turn it around. Five or six people. The autoway's straight for more than a quarter mile there; I can take off easily. Eugene probably has an airport."

"Lot of trouble to go look at some books," Rico said.

"Might as well use the plane while we can," Paul said. "Gonna be scrap metal in a few days."

"You think it's safe?" the pale elder said.

"No. But what is, nowadays?" He grinned at him. "As a plane, sure, it's safe enough. It got us to Russia and back, by way of Maryland. It can make it to Oregon. If nobody shoots it down, and the Martian power keeps working."

Her brow furrowed. "If the power went off, could you glide to a landing?"

"Maybe. There are emergency mechanical links to the control surfaces. But you have to find someplace flat, not too far away." He looked around at the mountains surrounding us. "It would drop really fast."

"So you would do it?" Rico said.

"Sure." He said that a little too fast. What, me afraid?

"We might ought to use it for something more useful than books," the other elder said.

"I could fly anywhere you want," Paul said.

"Not much we need," the pale one said. "Lead for bullets, primers, powder . . . all for reloads. You know of a place we could walk in and buy some. Or trade?"

"Not on this planet," Roz said. "Same with other survival stuff. Even if you could find it, what would you use for money?"

"Maybe we shouldn't fly anywhere," Rico said. "Don't remind people that we're up here. Self-sufficient and comfortable."

"For the time being," the pale one said.

A little girl walked onto the porch, looking apprehensive. She silently raised her hand.

"What is it, Bits?" Roz said tiredly.

"Someone wants to talk to this lady." She pointed at me. "The Mars lady?"

"Weren't you told not to answer the phone?"

"He isn't *on* the phone, Primus. He's on the cube."

"What does he look like?" I said.

"I think he's a zombie. He don't look real."

"Doesn't," Roz said. She took the child by the hand, and we followed them through the cafeteria smells into a dark room with high windows and a central cube. In it, the image of Spy.

"Kid here says you look like a zombie," Paul said.

"How perceptive. I'm not exactly alive."

"You're nearby," I said. No lag in his reply.

"Close enough. Cable. Did you have a nice flight?"

"It was eventful. As you must know."

He nodded. "You went to Russia and came back to the US, threatened to murder the president, and escaped to this bucolic paradise. Do you want to know whether the president's security people are after you?"

"Would you tell us the truth?" Paul said.

"Ask Epimenides. They are not after you. Things are somewhat confused back at Camp David, not to mention Washington, but if you went back, they might give you a medal."

"What about the president?" I said.

"Under house arrest, in a manner of speaking. The soldiers are negotiating via cell with their erstwhile enemies. It's all very chummy, democracy in action."

"Are we still going to lose power on Wednesday?" Roz said.

"As far as I know. Would you rather it be sooner?"

"Later would be nice," I said. "Like not lose it at all. If there's a lesson, we've learned it."

" 'Don't fuck with the aliens'? I suppose you have learned that. But I don't think it's actually a lesson. Someone wants to talk with you."

His image faded and was replaced with one I didn't at first recognize; he looked sort of like the pale elder, but with more hair, streaming in thick white Medusa locks. Then he spoke, without moving his lips: Moonboy, gaunt.

"You're looking well," he said.

While I was doing a sort of goldfish imitation, Namir found his voice: "Moonboy. You were frozen solid. You can't be alive."

The Others had chosen Moonboy to represent the human race in their deep-freeze zoo, even though he was not mentally or emotionally competent by our standards.

"I am more alive than any of you are, in terms of intellectual growth. I synapse faster, and my memory is not limited by organic considerations. I don't lose my temper anymore."

He still had a scar on his forehead from where Dustin had whacked him with a pool cue after Moonboy had broken his wife's nose.

"How are you any different from Spy? You're hooked up to the Others like him, and exist at their convenience."

"Our shared history makes me different. Your group once had a person who loved me."

"How do you feel about that?" Namir said. "The fact that Meryl is dead."

His eyes blinked slowly. I don't think he used them for seeing. "How could I feel things, Namir? As you pointed out, I'm long dead myself."

Not as dead as Meryl, I thought. My palms still stung with blisters from the shovel we used for her grave.

"I'm not just a mouthpiece for the Others," he said. "I can communicate with you in real time. When I'm speaking for them, I'll hold my hand up, like this."

He raised his right hand and left it up. "You present an interesting problem, the five of you whom we have met physically."

"How nice that we're interesting," Namir said.

"Along with what I, Moonboy, remember, there is a context"—he shook his head, frowning—"a universe of discourse? Between humans and the Others. That is not simply predator and prey."

"You can eat us?" Namir said. "That clears up a few things."

"I know that is just humor. I caution you against using it. You don't want me to misunderstand you."

Moonboy put his hand back down. "I can say whatever I want to you, but of course they overhear. Do you have any questions?"

"An obvious one," Paul said. "When the Others captured and froze you, we were all almost twenty-five light-years away from here. When they sent us back, it was as if no time had elapsed at all, but twenty-five years had passed on Earth."

Moonboy nodded. "Twice twenty-five, there and back."

"Was the transfer instantaneous to you? Or have you been thinking about things for a quarter of a century?"

"There is no plain answer. It did just take an instant, in the way you're measuring time. But I thought a lot while that was going on, in a way that I perceive time. I'm sorry that's not clear. Time itself is not what you think it is."

Actually, that was about as clear as he had been when he was last alive. But he had started to lose it after a couple of years aboard ship. Then he broke Elza's nose while they were having sex, and things went downhill fast from there.

In a way, that seemed like a couple of weeks ago. But I guess time is not what I think it is. "In what sense are the Others predators?" I asked. "How are we prey?"

"You offer the new," he said. "Any new organism does. But social creatures, who can communicate about their surroundings, add another dimension."

"So now the Others can leave us alone," Namir said, "since we're not new anymore."

"How you react to what's happening is always new. There is plenty left to happen."

"And after they've learned enough?" I said.

"When you had biology in school, you dissected a cat." I remembered talking with him about that, and nodded. "After you had learned enough about the cat, what did you do with it?"

"It wasn't a cat anymore."

"I suppose not." He faded away.

"That was informative," Namir said.

Spy appeared again. "This may not be the last time we want to talk to you. Please stay near a cube receiver, or carry a small one. It makes things simpler."

"After the power goes out?" Namir's fists were clenched.

"We can make do." He flickered and disappeared.

"I wonder if that means they'll eventually just go," Paul said. "Once they learn enough."

"Leaving us in pieces on the dissecting table," Namir said.

❀

We waited in the cube room for a few minutes, in case Spy had another afterthought. Then Paul and Namir went with two of the guys on GEVs, to clean up the jet, assuming it hadn't already been plundered. Paul said he'd scavenge the portable cube from the plane, to carry in case Spy wanted to make a call.

Meanwhile, the rest of us worked on domestic arrangements. There was a cabin with only one couple in it, and they moved out with more grace than I would've displayed. We managed to fit in three pallets and two beds, each large enough for two people who didn't mind touching. There was a rickety table with four chairs on the porch. The nearest toilet was a hundred meters away, but the room had a sink and three one-gallon jugs for carrying water. Rico found us an assortment of sheets, towels, and pillows.

We rested, waiting for the scavengers to return. I took a pallet on the floor, tired but not sleepy, glad to have a pillow.

Why had the Others contacted us? Just to make sure we knew they were watching? We would have been surprised if they weren't. I went over the short exchange with Moonboy in my mind.

They were using us to collect new experiences. Had they ever told us that before? I wished Snowbird was still with us. Or one of the yellow family, ideally. They had more direct contact with the Others, though I wasn't sure they understood them better.

We should call Snowbird, at Novisibirsk, and fill her in on every-thing that had happened. Wait until Namir comes back, to handle the Russian phone system.

Other than the stuff about collecting "the new," what had we learned? Don't joke with them; that was very useful. Moonboy claimed to experience time differently from us, but that's probably true of all dead people.

Speaking directly for, or as, the Others, what had he said? With his hand up. That there is a "universe of discourse" connecting us and them. Things that we share. As predator and prey? Then he put his hand down, after warning Namir about joking. Did they say anything else through him?

Of course, there's no reason to think Moonboy was telling the truth or, even if he was, it was for the purpose of helping us. Even before he died, it was hard to figure out what was going on in that unbalanced head.

I fell asleep and dreamed a memory of him on *ad Astra*, before he'd snapped. He was composing at the keyboard, which he'd al-ways done silently, with earphones. In the dream he was playing out loud, the same four-note sequence over and over, a look of terrible Beethovenian concentration on his unlined face. The notes never varied in volume or phrasing. Someone once said that was a func-tional definition of insanity: doing the same thing time and again, always expecting a different outcome.

❖

Dinner was a madhouse of cheerful disorganization. There was a big iron kettle of vegetable stew on an outdoor fire, and a smaller pot of deer-meat chili, peppery enough to make my eyes water. Plates of cornbread and biscuits.

Almost all of the eighty-nine people ate at the same time, mostly out on the porch or spilled onto the weedy lawn behind it. People drank yerba maté or a sugary drink with some citrus flavor. Everyone except the smallest children served themselves.

Eating with lots of people still made me nervous, after years on the cramped starship. But this rambunctious clan was easier than the formal dinners when we first returned, everybody staring at us and speculating.

Here, we were the invaders from outer space, and these folks rarely saw anyone outside their extended family. When the children stared, I just stared back.

I wondered about my own children—not the fifty-four-year-old twins I talked to through the Martian time-lag, just before we landed on Earth—but the youngsters who had grown up hardly knowing their mother. They'd been three and a half—not quite two ares—when I left on *ad Astra*. Their generation was all raised by professional parenters, so it wasn't child desertion, no matter what it had felt like at the time to me. I watched these women here, scolding and playing with and fussing over their offspring, and felt an emptiness that couldn't be there for Elza and Alba. No hole to fill.

But I wasn't even a biological mother, just a gene donor who had occasionally played with the results. How much greater the lack would be for the woman who carried a person inside her for nine months, had it pulled from her body and then watched it, an actual piece of her own flesh, acquire a separate personality and go out into the world. That would leave a hole.

We would never talk again. Never even breathe the same air, feel the same gravity.

They could read all about Paul and me, and presumably had. Every clinical detail of our stressed hothouse lives aboard the starship was available for inspection. Maybe *because* anyone could read it, they would leave it alone.

At least I wouldn't be entertaining observers with the interesting sexual geometries Elza and Meryl had experienced, assuming the public record was also a pubic record. But neither of them had children to be embarrassed by Mother's example.

The scavengers came back during dinner with the happy news that the plane seemed not to have been touched; it was still locked up unharmed. They brought the rest of the weapons and powder ammunition. (The elder named "Wham-O" was in charge of recycling ammunition, but he had run out of primers, a little metal thing that's pressed into the rear of the cartridge. Without that, the bullet won't go anywhere, so primers were at the top of some theoretical wish list. Along with U-235 and the philosopher's stone.)

Paul had the portable cube in a bright orange Sea Rescue knapsack. They also emptied out the jet's liquor cabinet, mostly full bottles of whisky, rum, gin, and vodka. Some had obviously sampled a bit on the way home, but had managed not to wreck the floaters.

There was a raucous vote as to whether the devil's brew ought to be saved, consumed on the spot, or destroyed. Some form of consensus wisdom prevailed, and they measured out one ounce apiece for each adult, and preserved an ounce for each child. The ones in their teens objected, but were somewhat mollified by the attraction of specialness: on their eighteenth birthdays, they would get something no one else could have.

I chose an ounce of rum, but gave it to Paul. Not that I didn't sort of want it. But it wouldn't relax me, and it did him.

Dustin had told us about a telescope that Wham-O maintained, an old thing they'd picked up at auction when Dustin was little. He had fond memories of looking through it at the stars and moon and planets. After dinner, we took candles out under the starry sky to the big shed where the machine was kept, on the other side of the cornfield.

The roof of the shed rolled off, squeaking into a rail frame, and there was the old machine, a long brass tube about a foot wide glittering in the candlelight. It was mounted on a heavy black cast-iron thing but was balanced exquisitely; you could move it around with a fingertip. We blew out all the candles, to preserve night vision.

Wham-O used a big brass key to wind a spring-driven clock mechanism that ticked and moved the tube so it would slowly track the stars.

He used a small telescope mounted on the side of the big one to point it. First we looked at Uranus, which he warned would not be too impressive, and that was an understatement. It was a little bluish green ball, shimmering in the dark, along with two faint stars he said were its brightest moons. Neptune wouldn't be up for a couple of hours, but there wasn't much to see there anyhow. Years ago, you could've seen its largest satellite, Triton, but the Others blew it up back in 2079. Warming up for the main act.

(Wham-O seemed personally offended that the Others had blown up Earth's Moon. That deprived him of the telescope's most impressive target.)

We looked at a couple of pairs of galaxies, faint, faraway ovals, and a brilliant double star, Gamma something. Then he pointed it to Mars.

I had to blink away tears. It wasn't at all like the familiar sight of its globe from orbit—this fuzzy ball was too orange and indistinct. But it was clear enough, the white polar cap and the dark "continent" of Syrtis Major, and the broad Hellas desert, under which the Martians were living. Lying in wait, a trap, though neither they nor we had had any reason to suspect that.

I went back to stare at it some more after the others had looked. Probably the last time I would see my home planet.

I allowed myself to hope that we still had children and grandchildren there; that the Others had let them keep the technology they needed to live and breathe. They had not been humane with us, but not sadistic either, in spite of what the popular press claimed.

More mysterious than mean. If that made any difference to the outcome.

We looked at some more faint fuzzballs, distant galaxies less impressive than we'd seen earlier, and some wisps of interstellar cloud. It wasn't boring, exactly, but the sky seemed full of bright stars that would be more interesting, and I wanted to see Mars again. I asked him about that, and he chuckled.

"Well, to tell you the truth, I want you all to be part of an experiment. I didn't want you to look at anything bright for a few minutes.

"You know how to find Polaris?"

Paul had showed us that; I let Elza answer. Just draw a line from the two stars, the "pointers," on the end of the Big Dipper's bowl.

"Look there and tell me what you see." Not much. Polaris was noticeably blue, but not very bright. The other stars in the Little Dipper were even dimmer, and hardly looked like a dipper at all.

Dustin noticed it first. "It's darker."

"That's right," Wham-O said. "Not a lot of stars around there. But what else?"

"No moonglow," he said. "There's . . . there's not as much lunar debris in that direction?"

"Not much at all. If you look in that direction with the telescope, the sky is noticeably blacker. It's been that way for a couple of days.

"Now look up there." I could just see him pointing. "Up by Gemini and Taurus, the Pleiades."

"It's a lot brighter up there," I said.

"Brighter than it used to be?"

"I'm certain of it," he said.

"So the dust is moving away from the celestial pole," Paul said, "toward the equator?"

"It looks that way to me."

"So we're going to wind up with a ring, like Saturn?" Dustin said.

"I don't know that much about astronomy. I just know how to use the telescope."

"Paul?" I said. He had a fresh Ph. D. in astrophysics.

"I didn't study the solar system much. But my instinct says it would take a lot longer. Millions of years, at least.

"The Earth might have had rings when it was younger; might

have had them and lost them several times. They weren't gravitationally stable, not with the Sun and Moon pulling at them."

"Saturn has moons with its ring," Dustin said.

"But they're not large compared to Saturn itself. The Moon was a quarter as big as the Earth."

"So now that it's not there," Wham-O said, "maybe the Earth can have a ring?"

"Worth keeping an eye on."

"So we could leave, right?" There was a spark of excitement in his voice. "Speaking as a space pilot . . . if all that crap was in a ring, you could just avoid it, couldn't you?"

"I guess in theory you could just power in or out. Aim your spaceship somewhere and go there. But in fact, you can't *not* be in Earth orbit. That orbit defines a plane that goes through the center of the Earth and would cut through the ring in two places."

"Can't you just, like, get on the North Pole and shoot straight up?"

"Sure, if you could get to the North Pole with a hell of a lot of fuel. Trade your horses and cows for some good sled dogs."

"I'll take it up with Roz."

Paul was lost in thought for a minute. "You *could* do it, you know. Spaceports are near the equator for economy; use the planet's rotation to add to launch speed. But if you *had* to launch from a pole, you could."

"You'd want electricity, though."

He shrugged. "Thought experiment. Big chemical fireworks, like Jules Verne. Besides, the power might come back."

"Once the Others are through playing with us," I said, which was the way a lot of conversations ended.

We lit a couple of the candles and walked back to the main house, quiet now with the children asleep. The adults were sitting around talking, drinking wine in the candlelight, rustic and romantic.

With a few unsubtle hints, Paul and I were allowed a bit of privacy in the cabin before the others came to bed.

I hadn't had time to think about how much I missed that part of him, being alone with him. He felt that, too. We joke about men's sexuality as if it were just stimulus and response and hydraulics. But Paul has always been gentle and sweet with me, maybe too gentle.

Not for the first time, I felt a little jealous of Elza, with her two men. Not so much Dustin—I guess I already have a philosopher. Namir was the big unknown, capable of who knows what. Strong, cabled arms; deep, troubled eyes.

# 11

The next morning, over breakfast of eggs and French-toast corn-bread, Roz made a proposition. "First, I've asked around, and everybody's in favor of asking you to join us." The two elders with her nodded in unison, like white-plumed birds.

"Rico must've taken some arm-twisting," I said.

"Not once he saw the riot gun. With the riot gun, he had to take you, Alba, and with you everybody else."

"Nice to be useful," she said.

"Speaking of useful . . . while the plane still flies, you have plans for it?"

"There are pluses and minuses for every possibility," Paul said. "I'd like to reconnoiter a big city, like LA, but we'd be vulnerable to ground fire. And I wouldn't want to leave it parked at an airport."

"We were talking about using it for resupply," Namir said. "Is there anything you have in abundance that you could trade in exchange for something you lack?"

"Most of the things we lack are luxuries, or rarities. Luxuries, forget it, but there are sophisticated medical supplies and equipment we would like to have on hand. If somebody wants to trade them for cider or jerky."

"Maybe in a few months," Namir said.

"We do have that strange offer," she said, "for books. Printed paper books."

"Far enough to fly?" Paul said.

"Eugene, Oregon. About 180 miles. I called them as part of this call-your-neighbor thing?"

"A long hike."

"I talked to them again last night, and they got all excited about your being so close.

"There's a funny guy there who has a big store called Lanny's Lending Library. Thousands, tens of thousands of paper books. He lends them out or sells them. They're suddenly worth a lot."

"Priceless," I said. How many books would just disappear once the cloud shut down?

"Lanny really wants to talk to you guys, about the Others and all. For an afternoon, with him, we can have all the books we can carry out. The seven of you and three of us."

"Couple of hundred books," Namir said. "Is it worth tying up the plane? When we could go raid a hospital or something?"

"The hospitals are probably all empty by now," I said. "The ones that aren't under armed guard."

"Besides," Alba said, "an old-fashioned medical book is going to be a lot more valuable than some diagnostic machine that has to be plugged in."

Paul stood up. "Let's just go do it. Before the plane's a useless relic." I was a little concerned about being up in the sky when it *became* a relic. But it wasn't going to get any safer.

We took two floaters out to the plane. The elders stayed on the ground, in favor of a couple of men to carry lots of books, Rico and a big young fellow called Stack. Paul had them sit in the front and rear of the plane, for balance.

We turned the plane easily with the floaters, which we left there with the elders. The plane rolled a short way and took off into a slight breeze and rose smoothly through the mountain pass.

Paul followed the autoway system east and north, through a few wisps of cloud. The Earthers were transfixed by the scenery. Only Rico had flown before, and that had been as a boy.

We descended after about a half hour, Paul following directions first from the plane's robot-voiced navigator and then from someone on the cell. He banked down toward a long green rectangle, a recreation area in the exurbs near Lanny's library.

Coming in from the south, we passed just over our welcoming committee: three military trucks next to a flagpole that had the American flag flying upside-down. Paul landed and then turned around and taxied up to them.

There were two men and a woman in military fatigues, looking pretty dangerous. I saw Paul slip a pistol under his tunic when he got up and slapped the button that dropped the staircase. Namir carried a laser rifle.

The soldiers, if that's what they were, welcomed us and helped us into the back of one of the trucks, which had two unpadded benches and a lot of dust.

There were spectators, maybe a hundred people on the other side of the fence. They were quiet and didn't shoot at us.

The truck had a canvas top and thick metal walls, the steel back door open for ventilation. The woman who was our driver said that Lanny's was only about ten minutes away. We took off between the two other trucks, which had gun turrets.

It was a bumpy fast ride, seven minutes on a straight road that turned twisty at the end.

Lanny's was one of dozens of identical blocky buildings which looked futuristic to me, shimmering and windowless. Roz dismissed them as "turn-of-the-century." Our destination had a big whitewashed wooden sign, with LLL stenciled on it in rainbow colors. A man who had to be Lanny was standing in the doorway, broad smile in a dark face framed with wild frizzy white hair. He half bowed and swept an arm to the open door. "Our visitors from outer space, welcome."

The inside was a kaleidoscopic junk pile of old-fashioned printed books, seemingly stacked in no particular order, the floor actually just a series of cleared walkways among the stacks. Books were shelved floor to ceiling on the walls, serviced by tall ladders on rollers, which looked precarious. Those books had a semblance of order, similarly bound sets stacked together.

The study at Camp David had the lawyer's obligatory wall-to-wall books, dusted but not opened from one generation to the next. Sometimes you saw the same thing in academic offices, back in my time, symbols of the continuity of scholarship rather than actual tools for learning.

Aboard *ad Astra* we had a short shelf of actual books, one of which Namir still carried with him, the volume of Shakespeare's sonnets bound in leather. His new wife had given it to him just before she died in Gehenna.

A sense of order did emerge, in that one area would be dominated by history books, another by cookbooks, or by mathematics or novels. Between chemistry and poetry there was a coffee machine surrounded by upholstered chairs. We settled in.

"I probably don't have much time to live," Lanny said, easing into an overstuffed recliner. "I have a heart chip and started having angina pains soon after the power went off." He waved that off like a mosquito. "But I've spent a life and fortune satisfying my curiosity about this and that, and don't see any reason to stop now."

An elderly white man in a tuxedo brought out a tray of cups and saucers and served each of us as Lanny talked. "I'm mainly curious about the Others, of course, and what direction you think this thing is going to go." He was looking at Namir.

"Well, it's the end of the world, no matter what they do. The old world is irretrievably gone. Even if they were to disappear and never come back."

"Something we could never know for sure," I said. "They can go away for ten thousand years, and come back to undo everything we've done. Anything we've done."

"In the name of self-protection," Paul said, "like this time. No defense against it."

"So we live from day to day," Lanny said, "as some of us have always done anyhow. Surviving to the next day will be more problematic soon. But that's always been the human condition."

"Yeah, but we used to be the masters of creation," Dustin said. "The pinnacle of evolution, the top of the food chain. Philosophically, that's the main difference the Others have made."

"Philosophy may be our big weapon now, Dustin," Namir said. "We're counting on you." And the doctorate he'd never used.

"Physical weapons just seem to annoy them," Lanny said. "Or do you have any ideas along those lines?"

Namir and Paul exchanged glances. "We never know when we're being listened to," Paul said quietly. "Maybe all the time. So you couldn't take them by surprise."

"How could they listen to you here?" Lanny said.

"Homeland Security could do it back in our day," Elza said, "from across the street, maybe from orbit. Bounce a coherent beam of light off the window and analyze the vibrations."

"No windows here," I said.

"Clear line of sight to the display window in front," she said, "so it would just be a matter of getting a signal out of the noise."

"They don't even need that, though," Paul said. "They want us to carry a cube everywhere." He held up the bright orange knapsack. "It's not supposed to be a transmitter, any more than the one at Funny Farm was. But they talked with us through that one."

"And back at the NASA motor pool," I said. "They managed to turn on a set without touching it. How do you do that?"

"Use a remote," Card said. "I mean, the circuitry is there. It's not magic."

"From orbit? Pretty sophisticated engineering," Paul said. "We don't have any idea what their limits are."

"Like, we know they can't go faster than the speed of light,"

Dustin said. "But they can handle time in ways we don't understand.

"Our trip back from their planet seemed to take no time at all, though almost twenty-five years passed on Earth. And it wasn't a subjective perception—the plants in our life-support system didn't die. If you think of the plant's physiology—or ours—as a slow clock, well, it barely ticked in those twenty-five years."

"How do you explain that?" Lanny said.

"That *is* fucking magic," Card said. "If you want an accurate name for it."

Justin laughed. "It'll be interesting to see what theoretical physicists do with it, mathematical physicists. They've only had a week to think about it, though. It might take another century."

"So in a way, they do go faster than the speed of light," Lanny said, "or you and your carrots and all did. You spent a quarter of a century and didn't grow a single gray hair."

"Maybe not 'faster' than light. Wish I'd paid closer attention in physics class," Paul said. "It seems to me that the only way you can travel at the speed of light is to stop time, somehow." He shrugged. "Photons don't age."

"And if you go faster than light," Dustin said, "time goes backwards; effect precedes cause."

"So what does that mean?" I asked. "Things happen before they start?"

"Hard to visualize," he admitted. As if he could draw a picture if he only had a pencil.

"If they can do that, there's no point in even trying to fight them," Lanny said.

"Assume they can't," Namir said. "Or if they can . . . subvert causality, we know that they don't use the power. Or haven't yet."

"Maybe they have," Lanny said. "Have they ever made a mistake?"

"Sure," I said. "They could have destroyed the whole human race, remember? If Paul hadn't stopped them."

"No disrespect, Paul, but there's another way to look at that. You flew their cosmic time bomb to the other side of the Moon, and saved us from that. But then what happened to the Moon? What if they tried it again today?"

"Good point," Paul conceded. "So they were testing us?"

"Or just scaring the shit out of us. Who knows why they do anything? It's like asking 'why did the earthquake hit San Francisco?' With all those people there."

"We have to assume they do things for a reason," Namir said.

"What does that mean?" Lanny said. "We can say 'the earthquake hit San Francisco because it was built on a fault line,' or 'God sent the earthquake to punish them for Chinese food,' or it happened because of all the gold mining. The reason you prefer depends on the information and prejudices you bring to the question. How much actual information do you have about them?"

"Mostly inference," Dustin said. "All they've actually said to us, you could put on a couple of screens. And some of that was deliberately misleading."

"Spy is a key, obviously," Paul said. "Assuming that, with all their powers, they can watch us anywhere, any time, then they don't really need him for information."

"He's a temporal interface," I said. "It's convenient for them to talk to us in real time, our time."

"You did converse with them once," Lanny said. "When you were out at their star?"

"We had Spy then," I said. "We'd say something and wait for several minutes while they answered, through him."

"It would take them a couple of minutes to just say yes or no," Dustin said. "The more complicated responses wouldn't take much longer, but they apparently had billions of things pre-recorded, so it was just a matter of hitting the right billion switches."

"A lot of bases to cover," Lanny said.

"They think a lot faster than we do," he said. "Faster than we can imagine thinking, Fly-in-Amber said. He was the other Martian with us when we went to meet them. The resident expert on the Others."

"He knew next to nothing," Paul said. "As opposed to nothing."

"That was frustrating," I said. "Like all the Martians in the yellow family, he was born with an ability to communicate with the Others—"

"Born with the knowledge of their language?"

"Weirder than that. More like being born with a sixth sense, which you're unaware of until it's triggered." I tried to remember how he had described it. "He didn't make any sense out of the Others' message himself. He said it was like being able to speak the language perfectly, but only as a mimic. Like a parrot."

"Are any of the Martians up in Russia in the yellow family?"

"None that we met," I said, "and no way we can talk to them on Mars."

I missed what anybody might have said then. My mind went a little haywire, realizing I could see Mars in the evening sky—could see light from the planet where my family and friends lived—and so could talk to them, in theory. But theory wasn't practice; communications satellites were dust. They would all grow old and die without me.

Or might be dead already, along with all the Martians and other humans in Mars, if the Others had pulled the plug on them.

I should have asked Spy. And then wonder whether to believe his answer.

The white butler came back to refill our coffee, and produced a flask of brandy when Elza asked for something stronger. That led to some chat about living conditions aboard *ad Astra*, which reminded me to be grateful for gravity, and coffee that came from actual beans, made with water that had never passed through a kidney.

"Coffee may be more valuable than the books," Lanny said. "I took delivery on two tons of roasted beans on 28 April, the day before they pulled the plug. The basement's full."

"Make everyone who buys a cup of coffee buy a book," Dustin said.

"Paying with what?" Paul said.

Lanny shook his head. "Barter gets complicated fast. Especially with books. I can trade you one poem for another, or two small ones for a big one. But how many for a chicken, and where do I put the chicken?"

"In the first stanza," Elza said. "Or maybe that's the egg."

He ignored that. "We're pretty much on the barter system now, but it's money-based. You bring in twenty dollars' worth of books, and I'll give you ten dollars' worth in trade, or five dollars in cash. Phasing out the actual cash, but it's still a unit of exchange."

"What about California bucks?" Roz said, smiling.

"Useful for personal hygiene." The governor of California had authorized the printing of paper money, backed in some arcane way by the state's natural resources. None of it had made its way to Funny Farm.

Lanny pulled a wad of bills out of his front pocket and sorted through them. "I did take one yesterday; gave him ten cents on the dollar. Here." It was greener than the others, labeled ONE HUNDRED CALIFORNIA DOLARS. There was a picture of a rugged-looking man in a cowboy hat, identified as Ron Reagan. Small print said it was legal tender anywhere in the universe.

"That will be handy," Paul said, "once we have this business with the Others straightened out. California oranges in grocery stores all over the galaxy."

"Governor was a fucking nut-case even before this all happened. Like I have to tell you guys."

"He used to be the funniest thing on the cube," Roz said. "He didn't just want to secede from the States. He wanted to put California into orbit, and declare independence from Earth."

"Not really?" I said.

"Science wasn't his strong suit. His handlers said it was metaphor. Everybody knew better."

We talked for a couple of hours, satisfying Lanny's curiosity about our flight out to Wolf 25 and meeting with the Others. About half the time we just talked about our remote pasts, growing up in the last half of the twenty-first century.

The Others first made their presence known almost sixty years ago. There aren't too many people around who remember everyday life as adults back then, without a Sword of Damocles hanging in the sky. Back when there was "everyday life," uncomplicated by doom.

Lanny said that suicide had been the leading cause of death for as long as he could remember, for children as well as adults. He was born in 2068, right after Gehenna. His Jewish mother killed herself before he was one. He grew up with his father's fierce atheism and had never been tempted away from it.

He led us around the store with a shopping cart. Roz had a scribbled list of all the titles in Funny Farm's library.

Some choices were obvious, like medical manuals and a five-volume gold mine, the *Foxfire Journals*, a twentieth-century compendium of low-technology solutions to the problems of country living, from midwifing to burial. Chicken raising, building a smokehouse, foraging for wild plants, how to make a banjo. That got Namir's interest. He'd made a balalaika to pass the time on the starship, but left it in orbit, to be sent to Earth later. Pulverized now.

Lanny unlocked a glass case and gave us a fat one-volume *Medical Practices* from 1889, before antibiotics. Some of the medicine seemed more superstition than science; the surgery, painful butchery.

How long would our anesthetics hold out? Long enough for me to die before needing them?

Paul chose a judicious assortment of books on science and engineering, and Lanny gave him a thing called a "slide rule," along with a fragile yellowing folder of instructions. It was a foot-long slab of yellow metal with numbers printed all over it. Paul squinted at it and moved the middle bar around and told me the cube root of 100 was 4.64. I supposed that might come in handy some day.

By mutual consent, we all got to choose two books without argument. I got the fat old poetry book that had sustained me the year before my family moved to Mars, Palgrave's *Golden Treasury*, and a one-volume complete Shakespeare in tiny print. Roz's list already had a Shakespeare, but Rico said it was a simplified edition for children.

About half the cart was filled with children's books, a mixture of schoolbooks and play. Raising kids without the cube was going to be a challenge. I had a disturbing vision of myself as an old lady, scaring children with stories around the campfire. Though they wouldn't be so easy to scare by then.

One priceless find was a thirty-volume set of *Encyclopedia Britannica*, from 2031. It had been a curiosity, not for sale, but when the cloud evaporated, *it* would be all we had. A finger-powered paper memory bank. I decided to read through it, five pages a day. That would be eighty-four hundred days, so when I finished I would be twenty-three years older and wiser.

There was a whole section of survival manuals, mostly earnest and useless, either painfully obvious or relying on technology we used to think was basic. There was a Girl Scout manual, *Handbook for Girls*, that had useful tips about getting along in the woods. For a fun week away from home.

What we really needed was a book about how to rebuild civilization from scratch, but if there was one, it was checked out.

Lanny had a good idea, a practical use for his printing press. Try to boil down everything that made Funny Farm work, and everything they'd done wrong, and print it on a single sheet of paper, both sides. Send copies up and down the coast, and out into the Plains, so that people wouldn't have to reinvent the wheel.

We sat down and, with Lanny's help, made a chart covering the benefits civilization provided. He traced it on a three-foot flatscreen, drawing circles around words with his finger while a teenaged boy drew a copy on a piece of paper with a pencil. It did look odd, but paper was going to be *it* soon. We'd better be learning how to make the stuff.

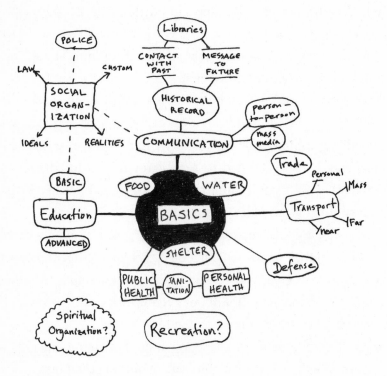

After about twenty minutes, we all ran out of ideas and looked at the thing quietly. Something important was missing.

"Where is art?" I said.

Rico looked at me quizzically. "Who?"

"There's no place there for art . . . or science."

"Or philosophy," Dustin said. "All that comes later."

"She has a point," Lanny said. "If all you do is plant crops and haul water and keep a roof over your head, and fight off the other savages, what are you?"

"Successful savages," Namir said. "You'd rather be a cultured corpse?"

"To be realistic," Roz said, "how much art and science did we get done at the farm?"

"How much did we need?" Rico said. "We aren't exactly an art colony. And we had the cube to keep up with science."

"Had," Roz said. "Maybe art will take care of itself. People do draw and paint and make music. But science and technology . . . what will it be like a hundred years from now? When everybody who ever got a degree in science is dead?"

"I guess you want general textbooks about every discipline," Lanny said, "and then be selective about advanced texts."

"Civil engineering," Dustin said, "which we used to call a contradiction in terms. Buildings, roads, sewers. Chemical engineering rather than pure chemistry. That kind of selectivity."

"We can take all the time you need," Lanny said.

"We're not going to find paper books that are up-to-date on technology," Paul said. "I didn't have any when I got my degree back in '63."

"Same at the university here," Lanny said. "If you want to look at a paper book in the library now, you have to go to the reserve room or Special Collections, and wear gloves. The only new paper books I see here are gift items or things that were printed for collectors.

"Library books are how I started this store. The university library was selling off books by the pound when they went paperless, back in '21."

"During the big depression," the butler said.

"Yeah; my dad had made a fortune in real estate. When he died, I got this building and enough money to fill it with books." He laughed. "It was 2121, and I had just turned forty-two. Not that I'm superstitious."

I thought the world economy was under central control before 2121. Would there be an economics book printed later than that? *A Child's Garden of Macroeconomics?*

Lanny led us around the store with the paper copy of the diagram and helped us choose old academic books that weren't outdated or too fragile to be of use. There was a debate over electronics and computer science. Justin thought they were about as useful as a "how to wrap a mummy" book. But they compromised on a couple of general texts and a wall chart full of arcane symbols.

I have some sympathy for Paul's side, the sciences, even though I'm a useless liberal-arts type myself. How could anybody decode all that stuff from scratch? Maybe the electricity would come back in a hundred years.

People might remember how to turn on the lights, or the machines, but who could repair or replace them?

A uniformed soldier came rushing in, and saluted Lanny. "Sir, California has . . . they bombed the border."

Lanny was incredulous. "The Oregon border?"

"All of it, they said. Hellbombs, all along the state's borders."

Hellbombs gave off intense radiation for years, without causing any other damage.

"'California for Californians,'" Lanny quoted. "Are they far enough away not to harm us?"

"You could detect it, sir, but just barely. We measured one or two milligrays. Ten times that wouldn't hurt."

"He threatened this during the last election," Alba said, "but we thought it was just isolationist rhetoric."

"Could he have enough bombs to actually do it?" Justin asked. "He'd need to drop one every five miles or so."

"Their standard radius of effectiveness is about five miles," Namir said, "so one every ten miles would do it."

"You can fly above them?" Rico asked.

"No problem," Paul said. "Hell, you could drive past one in a car, a mile or two away, if you were going fast enough."

"And didn't want to have children," Namir said. "You'd get quite a sunburn, a mile away."

"Nobody's going to walk across the border," Paul said, "or settle near it. I assume Fruit Farm is far enough away."

"Unless he tossed one our way," Rico said.

"Not likely," Roz said. "He's crazy, but he's sort of *our* crazy. Back to basics and all."

"With his mansion in Malibu," Rico said. "I wonder if he bombed the border with the Pacific."

"He didn't, sir," the soldier said. "Just the borders with other states and Mexico."

"That's great," I said. "If the plane doesn't work, we can hijack a boat."

Paul was shaking his head. "Shit. What do we have? Roz, how badly do you guys want to go back?"

"You could make a good case for going anywhere else," she admitted, "but no; it's our home." She looked at the other three and got dour nods. "I guess we're at your mercy."

"Oh, I'll give you a ride. But what do the rest of us do? Stay stuck in California for years, or get out while we can?"

"Will the hellbombs still work after Wednesday?" I asked.

"Nothing electrical in them," Namir said.

There was an awkward pause. "You couldn't stay here," Lanny said. "You'd more than double our population."

"Funny Farm would probably be the best place for you," Roz said, and pointed to the center of the diagram. "Food, water, and shelter."

I felt a rising choking panic. Stuck on a few acres of farmland? After having two worlds and parsecs of space to roam in?

Paul gave me a look that I couldn't read. What did *he* want—a life of kids and crops and chores?

"I think we ought to go," he said slowly. "Let's get these books on the ground, on the other side. Then decide whether to stay or go . . . someplace."

My mind was spinning, or rather rattling around like a pebble in a can. Even if it was my choice, I wouldn't know what to do. Return to the farm, stay in Eugene, head for the sea, the hills? Funny Farm was a haven and a trap. Hiding place and target.

Well, we did have to go there, Step One. Maybe then take off and head back east? Rather than stay locked up in a radioactive lunatic asylum.

Lanny helped us pack the books into cloth and plastic bags, with the store's logo, RESERVED FOR VOLUME CUSTOMERS. We turned on the cube and saw the governor's ranting speech while we loaded the truck and rolled off to the field.

The watching crowd was bigger. Some of them shouted at us as we slowed to go through the gate. But they weren't armed, or at least weren't shooting.

I couldn't blame them for being resentful. But we weren't actually escaping. Just hopping from one part of the frying pan into another.

We stacked the bags of books evenly into the overhead racks. The cargo area was pretty full with the weapons, ammunition, food, and water we'd brought. Even if we had carried it from the Farm and back for nothing, it had been reassuring.

When the door eased shut and cut off the crowd noise, I relaxed. The rush of the jet exhaust was comforting. We bumped along the soft ground for half a minute and then floated up into the air.

"Need to get some altitude," Paul said over the intercom. "Like to be a few miles up when you go over the bombs." He'd mentioned that on the way out. Hellbombs fall in such a way that their radiation isn't wasted on the sky; most of it's reflected to fan out horizontally. But it was still significant a mile or so up; besides, a bomb could land on a slant or tip over.

The plane didn't have a radiation detector. If our skins started to blister, we'd know something was wrong.

Paul said we were at fifteen thousand feet, over four kilometers, when we approached the California border.

It was easy to see where the hellbombs had been dropped. A

black spot that lightened to a brown circle, then yellow, fading into green.

The governor had given his citizens one hour of warning. Plenty of time to get away at a fast walk, unencumbered by possessions.

A couple of minutes after we crossed the border, the flatscreens on the chair backs blinked into life. Spy appeared, smiling wanly.

"The Others have decided that this phase of the experiment is over. You might start looking for a place to land." It went blank, and at the same time, the jet's engine stuttered and stopped.

Paul looked back down the aisle. "Belt in tight. Be ready to assume the crash position before we hit. I mean 'land.'"

"'Crash position'?" Rico said.

"Feet together, knees together." He turned back to the controls and shouted, "Hands on your knees! Get your head down!"

"And kiss your ass goodbye," Dustin said.

# 12

The plane went into a sickening bank, dropping at a steep angle, and then bobbed up with a lurch and glided on the level for a while. Not really level; I could see individual trees growing larger by the minute. The air shriek grew louder and deeper in pitch. I couldn't see what Paul might be aiming for. It was all forest and rolling hills underneath me.

We later learned that Paul was aiming for the town of Holstock, which was the only urban area visible when Spy told us they were pulling the plug. It was a couple of miles too far away, though.

There was still no road visible when I saw the plane's shadow rushing up to meet us, and obediently assumed the proper position, bent over with hands and eyes and anus clenched tight. He was aiming for a short bit of country road that ran straight for a fraction of a mile.

We hit the gravel road hard, with an explosion as both tires blew. Looking at the path later, you could see that we skidded spraying gravel for less than a hundred yards, and were still going pretty fast when the left wingtip hit a tree. We spun half around and the other wing dug into the ground, and the plane cartwheeled twice and crashed into a pine forest.

All I remember is my face hitting the viewscreen, which didn't break. I think I was only unconscious for a minute or so. Woke up aching all over, blood trickling off my chin from a cut over the cheekbone. My mouth was full of blood; upper and lower incisors had ripped into my lips. My left eye was swollen shut, and blood trickled down from my left knee. I smelled pine. The plane ticked and squeaked.

Shoulders felt bad, but my hands worked. I opened the seat-belt clasp and tried to stand. The plane was canted over at about a thirty-degree angle. Behind me, I could see that a thick branch or small tree had punched through a window. That was Alba's seat, and she was obviously dead. So was the man across from her, one of the Funny Farm volunteers, his head at a drastic angle, chin torn off.

I picked my way forward, bracing myself to find Paul dead. There was very little light up there, the windshield and side windows buried in green.

Paul was hanging from his straps, his face a mask of blood. But when I touched him he groaned.

"Paul? Paul, can you hear me?"

One eye blinked open, startling white against the red. He rubbed both hands over his face and stared at the blood. "What the fuck . . . Do we have casualties?"

"I don't know—yes. Two, at least."

"Help me here." He was trying to undo the clasps on his harness, fingers slippery with blood. When they clicked open, he rolled half onto me.

He felt his head gingerly. "Where the fuck is my flight helmet?"

It was down by his feet. I handed it to him, and he twisted the microphone around. "Mayday. Mayday." Then he shook his head, hard, and threw it away.

I helped him to his feet. "Sorry, sweetheart," he said, "not enough road." We looked back down the aisle.

In the back, Namir was crunched over Dustin, giving him mouth-to-mouth. Roz lay unconscious or dead across the aisle. Card had a cut on the top of his head; Elza was dabbing at it with a tissue, her other arm hanging limp at her side.

"Where's Rico?" Paul said.

"Under the seat up here," Elza said. "He slid."

"Tobogganed," Paul muttered. I followed him up there and saw the body. He either hadn't fastened in properly or the belt failed. His body had slid under the seat in front of him, but his chin caught on the bottom of the chair, and his head stayed behind.

He didn't look real, and neither did the other man, Stack, his jaw taken away. His eyes were open but there was no life in them.

Paul was kneeling over Roz, his ear to her chest. "Heart's beating. Find some water?" He crawled up to Namir and Dustin. I found a water bottle and broke the seal.

Tried to pour some into Roz's mouth, but it just dribbled out. When I splashed some on her face, though, she reacted, wincing a little.

"Are you okay?" Brilliant question.

She opened one eye. "Yeah, but you look like shit." She coughed and propped herself up on her elbow. "Think I broke a rib." She coughed into her hand and looked at it. "Not too serious. How is Rico?"

"Dead. He's dead."

She shook her head. "God, Rico. Anybody else?"

"Stack, Alba, maybe Dustin."

"Do we want to get out of this damn thing before it explodes?"

"Not a problem," Paul said, not looking back. "Runs on helium."

It was all Martian magic, of course; it could probably run on mushrooms. I made my way back to the cockpit area and hit the red door button several times. My knuckles were raw and bleeding on both hands. "The door doesn't work."

"See if you can pull the rubber strip off one of the windows. The one over the wing there." Roz had longer fingernails, so she was able to pick it away. There was a red ribbon along the bottom that said PULL AND KICK in various languages. We both pulled on the ribbon and it made a click sound. I punched the window out with a single kick, and it whacked my shin on the way down.

"Get out there with a weapon," Namir said, gasping. He'd just stopped giving Dustin mouth-to-mouth. "We'll have company."

"Is Dustin?" I said.

"He's breathing," Namir said, and slid an assault rifle down the aisle. I picked it up and painfully got my head and one shoulder through its strap. Got both legs through the window, dropped onto the broken wing, and slid to the ground. Managed not to poke the rifle barrel into the dirt.

Some bird chirped in a long, monotone scold, but otherwise there was only a sigh of wind in the pines and the wreck's small metallic noises. Hot-metal smell and newly turned earth.

I stepped away a few paces and could see our path of destruction. Saplings snapped off, pointing this way. Three deep gouges in the forest loam. From this low angle, I couldn't see the road Paul had aimed for.

Rico and Stack dead, maybe Dustin. Probably no medical help any closer than Funny Farm. More than fifty miles away, in some direction.

"Don't shoot?" It was a woman's voice, not far away.

"I won't," I said. "Where are you?"

A gray-haired woman in a brown shift stepped out from behind a dense bramble. "You have a plane wreck?"

No, this is the way we like to land. "The power went out. The Others turned it off a couple of days early."

She looked at a watch on her wrist and nodded. "First the god damned governor and now the god damned aliens. Be an earthquake next. You from NASA?"

I still had the coveralls on, though they wouldn't pass inspection, blood and all. "No. I was their guest." That was inane, or at least inadequate.

"Other survivors on the plane?"

I nodded. "Some injured. Is there a hospital?"

"Town's six, seven miles. Come up to the place, though. We have a cabin down the road here, get you cleaned up." She stepped forward and offered her hand. "Germaine Lerner."

I shook her hand and was relieved that she didn't recognize my name. "Others who need more than just cleaning up. Help me with them?"

"See what we can do." She was about my age—thirties, not eighties—and stout and muscular.

When we got back to the plane, Roz was resting at the base of the tree, and Namir was on the ground, helping Paul lower Dustin down the wing. Dustin was awake but pale.

"We think broken ribs and collarbone," Namir said. "Hello?"

Germaine introduced herself. "We can make him a pallet on the floor. I'm afraid my husband has dibs on the bed. He's doing poorly."

"What's wrong?" I asked.

"He was coming back from town on a motorcycle when the bombs dropped. He didn't wipe out, but he got burned by it."

"How close was he?" Namir said. "To where it went off."

"I don't know. It's not like they make an explosion. Close enough he felt the heat inside his body."

He winced. "There might be some radiation medicine in the plane's first-aid kit. He ought to go to a hospital, though."

"Urgent care center's closer. I suspect there'll be a lot of people there." She stepped up and put her arm around Dustin, guiding his arm around her shoulder. "Come on, now."

Paul slid down the wing, pretty spry and looking a little better, most of the blood wiped off his face. Elza backed clumsily out of the window, her left arm in a sling improvised from a shirt.

"Card will be all right," she said to me. "He's dizzy, and I told him to rest for a bit."

"I'll come back for him," I said. "Let's follow Germaine to her place and take stock."

"I'll wait here," Namir said, easing down against the wing, propping his machine gun in easy reach. "We'll need a shovel if you have one."

"Got two," Germaine said. "Take care of the living first." She walked off, easily supporting Dustin, following an invisible trail.

Their cabin was only a few minutes' walk. It blended in well with the woods. Up close, you could see that the rough-hewn logs were fading plastic. Two three-wheeled motorcycles were parked in front, giving off an odd smell I remembered from childhood. "Those run on gasoline?"

"When we can find it. There's a place in Yreka sometimes has it. Let me go in first." I took Dustin from her. She pounded on the door three times and then opened it slightly. "Don't shoot, it's me. We got company."

The man inside said something unintelligible. "That was a plane crash we heard." She opened the door and stood in the doorway. "Some people hurt."

He came out of the darkness and stood next to her, peering out, holding a shotgun. "You in the plane that dropped them bombs."

"That wasn't us," Paul said.

"It was somebody, sure as hell." The muzzle of the gun moved to point in our general direction.

"I'm a doctor," Elza said. "I should look at those burns."

"What burns?"

"The left side of your face. Germaine says you passed close to a hellbomb."

"Nothing you can do about that."

"Maybe I can." She walked toward him, and he put the gun

down inside the door. She held his hair aside and studied his skin. Put the back of her hand against his cheek. "Does this hurt?"

"No. A little."

"Sick to your stomach?"

"A little."

"You ought to lie down and rest." To Germaine: "The care center should have oral marrow stimulant. Just to be on the safe side. Tell them he got close enough for a sunburn."

She nodded. "God damn governor."

The man muttered something about him being a good man anyhow, and she rolled her eyes. "Go lie down."

"We'd better get to that care center ourselves," Elza said. "Is that in Yreka?"

"No, just down the road in Holstock. I guess a couple hours, walking, though. Six or seven miles. Come in and get a drink first."

We followed her in through the door. The cabin was a neat single room with two beds, two chairs, and a table. Boxes of food and dry goods, and a case of ammunition, opened.

"My grandfolks bought this place back in '79, when the Martians first came." She crossed to a sink and pumped a handle vigorously several times, and water gushed out. She filled the four glasses that were on the sink.

"So you were on NASA business in that plane?"

"We were trying to get to Funny Farm," Roz said. "You know where that is?"

"Kind of. Never been there. Now that's gonna be a walk." She handed out the glasses.

"You know which way we go?" Paul took a sip and passed me his glass.

"I've been up that way," the man said. "Give me the map."

She got a plastic map from the table drawer and he unfolded it. He rubbed it for magnification, but, of course, nothing happened.

"Lucky it has a picture at all," he muttered, and put a thick finger down in the middle of nowhere. "You follow the gravel road about three mile, where it makes a T with a two-lane. Go to the right, and it takes you into Holstock. Urgent care is there on the main street. Don't know what you gonna pay with."

"We'll sort that out with them," Roz said. "From there we go south?"

"Not unless you're a bird. Crossroads in the middle of town, that's County 2031. You might want to go north, to the left. Right would take you down to Yreka. I heard gunfire there and turned around."

"But left goes up to the border."

"Yeah, you don't want to go that far." He leaned close to the map, where he had his finger down. "Black dotted line here, that's a fire road, gravel, won't be marked. You follow it eight or ten mile, you get to the autoway, 241."

"Which is where we took off from, this morning." Paul studied it and pointed to where a blue line crossed 241. "That's the river that goes by Funny Farm." It was about an inch away. "What is that, fifty miles?"

"Forty, anyhow. Pretty hilly."

"We have a lot of empty jugs," I said. "Mind if we fill them up here?"

"Course," she said. "You have food up at Funny Farm?"

"Eighty acres planted," Roz said.

"Well, you can take some of ours to get there," she said, "but you remember us, right? We might be knocking on your door one day."

"We'll remember," Roz said. "I guess that's the way of the world now."

"The Lord helps them that helps themselves," she said, staring at Roz. "But we are all His instruments."

❋

We emptied the plane wreck of everything that would be of value to us or our hosts. We pried out the executive folding bed from behind the cockpit for them; besides the water, they gave us a box of dehydrated emergency meals, enough to feed us all for several days. After that, I guess we'd have to shoot a deer or catch some fish. Germaine gave us some line; both Namir and Dustin knew something about fishing.

Paul insisted that I not help with the grave-digging, and I didn't protest much. My palms were raw. Elza had snipped away the flaps of skin and dressed them with gauze.

I helped wrap Alba and Rico and Stack in blue NASA blankets, while the others used pick and shovel to carve holes out of the root-laced soil.

There was some grisly discussion of the riot gun and Alba's thumb. For it to fire, it had to read her thumbprint on the pistol grip. We didn't know whether the sensor would work without power. Namir studied it, though, and used a screwdriver and hex wrench to disable it. The thing would only fire single-shot, but how many shots would you need?

She had been Christian, so we improvised a cross marker and Germaine read from the Bible. Rico and Stack were atheists, but Roz quoted Buddha for them, for their journey.

Our own journey shouldn't be long delayed, but we were all exhausted, and the sun was going down. Elza and Dustin, with their broken bones, got Germaine's discarded bed. We gave Card the pallet Germaine had made for Dustin. Elza had managed to stitch up his head wound one-handed, with my help.

Card didn't seem too badly hurt, but he hadn't said two words, and he didn't seem to follow conversations. Maybe he was dwelling on his other personalities, still as dead as Alba and Rico and Stack.

I took a cup of tea out to where he was sitting alone on the cabin porch. He didn't respond when I set the tea down next to him.

"Almost too much to handle," I said.

"Almost?" He made a ghastly smile, a grimace. "I thought that nothing I would ever do would be crazier than Mars. Maybe it wasn't Mars, though—maybe it was *you*. I had a nice, quiet life until you came back into it. Now everything is completely fucked up and confusing and people are dying left and right!"

"Drink the tea, Card."

"But it's true! If you hadn't stumbled on the Martians they'd still be hiding underground, and we wouldn't have the Others fucking with every fucking thing."

"They were right next door. If I hadn't stumbled onto them, someone else would."

"But someone else didn't. You're to blame for the whole fucking shooting match."

It's not as if I had never followed that line of reasoning myself. "So what do you suggest I do?"

He wiped away tears. "If you had a time machine, you could go back and kill yourself before it started."

"Sure, that would work."

"This might." He reached into his jacket pocket and pulled out a revolver.

I jumped back. "Card!"

"Oh, don't worry." He put the muzzle of the gun to his temple and laughed. "Watch." He pulled the trigger and it made a loud click.

"You should see your face."

I couldn't think of anything to say or do. He took out a box of bullets and fumbled six into the cylinder, dropping two but ignoring them. He put the gun back into his pocket and, tears streaming past a smile, started up the path toward the wreck and the graves.

For a couple of minutes I stood there on the edge, waiting for a single shot. Paul came out onto the porch.

"Where is your brother?"

"I don't know," I said. "I'm not his keeper."

# 13

About halfway through my second watch, I saw something curious. At first I thought it was a bright, slow meteor among all the streaking lights. But it didn't go out. It shone steadily until I lost it in the trees to the north. An old satellite?

Card didn't come back that night or the next morning. I told people he'd seemed depressed, but didn't elaborate. Paul obviously knew there was something more to it, but didn't press me.

When Paul woke up, I mentioned the light I'd seen in the sky.

"Wouldn't be a satellite," he said. "It was going south to north?"

"I'm sure of it." It was in the Big Dipper when it disappeared in the trees.

"Can't be an artificial satellite; they're all long gone. Maybe an Earth-grazing asteroid; they can have eccentric orbits." He explained about the plane of the ecliptic, and I sort of understood.

"More likely, it's something that belongs to the Others. Something rocks bounce off, or protected by a force like a floater's pressor field."

"That would work, up in orbit?"

"Who knows? No way to get up and find out."

"Maybe it came from Mars," I said. "If the Others didn't take their power away."

Elza was listening. "Or maybe it's from Heaven. Baby Jesus finally decided to step in and help us out."

"If Mars had power and could send a ship to Earth," Paul said, "why would it be over here? They'd send it to Washington or London or someplace."

"We're here," I said. "Martians."

"But there's no way for them to know that," Elza said. "Not that there's anything wrong with hoping."

✺

We waited until the sun cleared the mountains to the east. "Card knows where we're going," Namir said. "We mustn't wait any longer."

I wasn't going to disagree, and after his scene at the wreck, I probably wasn't alone in hoping we'd seen the last of him. And none of the others had last seen him down the barrel of a gun.

We still had the NASA mail cart, though it wasn't very efficient on gravel. We had to cull through the books, leaving half of them with the Lerners. The ones we kept leaned heavily toward children's books and general references like the Britannica set.

In exchange for all the books, they gave us one of the shovels, a folding campers' model called an entrenching tool. I hoped we wouldn't need it.

We did carry all the ammunition, and enough weapons so everyone had at least one. Namir carried the riot gun and a pistol. Elza, with only one arm functional, carried the other pistol and two bandoliers of machine-gun ammunition for Paul's weapon. I had an assault rifle and a machete.

I hoped we looked too dangerous to attack. More dangerous than I felt. Besides the rifle strapped across my back and the machete bumping my leg, I had two gallons of water hanging front and back, and the encyclopedia from CAM to FRA, three volumes, in a cloth bag under my right arm. From CAMera to FRAternity I couldn't be beaten, though in a gunfight I might be a little slow.

The cart made noise, crunching through the gravel, and it really took two people to haul it along efficiently. So we wound up moving it in shifts: two of us would stay with it, along with another guard, while the other three, plus Germaine, moved quietly forward. They would signal when the coast was clear, and we'd drag the load up to join them. Then switch teams, Germaine always in front, in case we met neighbors.

It actually wasn't too inefficient, with everybody resting half the time and moving pretty fast otherwise.

We picked up speed when we reached the T and turned into a paved road. We made steady progress for about an hour, and then ran into people.

We saw each other from a long way off. They stopped and waited for us, nervous, outnumbered and outgunned.

Two men, two women, and a baby. One of the men was old and the other looked worse than Mr. Lerner, radiation burns on both bare arms and face. Haggard and ill-looking.

Paul spoke to them as we approached. "Hello. You were caught on the border?"

The older man was leaning on a rifle, perhaps trying to look casual. "The boy here was. He drove home, but now the car doesn't work."

"Where you headed?"

"Yreka. Place in Holstock said they didn't have anything for radiation."

"Going the long way," Germaine said.

"They told us not to take 2031. You'd best not, either. Some gangers got the road blocked." Good thing we were headed the other way.

"Goddamn Crips," Germaine said. "Think they own the road."

"Huh uh," the young man said. "This is a car gang. If it was Crips I could walk through." He pulled up his T-shirt to reveal an elaborate dragon tattoo on his chest.

That must have meant something to Germaine. She nodded. "No radiation meds in Holstock?"

"Sent us to Yreka."

"I'll come along, you don't mind. My old man got burned, too."

"I know you," the man with the rifle said to me. "You're that woman from Mars."

I almost said yeah, people say I look like her, but the NASA clothes were kind of conspicuous.

"Does us a lot of good," Paul said, facing the man.

He nodded slowly, perhaps taking in Paul's munitions. "Sure, come on along," he said to Germaine.

"Good luck getting home," she said to Roz, and gave me a confused look. Woman from Mars? They walked away slowly, not looking back.

It took another hour and a half to get into Holstock. We encountered two other small groups, though others may have watched from hiding. Those two saw us and ran into the woods.

The residential area of the town was a few blocks of individual homes mixed with condos, along with hotels and guest houses. The commercial part of town began abruptly, stores with a curious uniformity of design and apparent age. Germaine said that was because about a generation ago, most of the town was consumed in a runaway forest fire.

There was a short line, five people, waiting outside the care center; six more on chairs inside. A nurse came out with a piece of paper taped to an otherwise useless notebook. She was a pretty girl in a white uniform, brightly clean, bisected by a thick belt holding up a heavy pistol in a low-slung holster.

She was not surprised that we didn't have any California dollars, and accepted a box of dehydrated rice and Thai chicken as "symbolic down payment." Roz signed a two-paragraph document that said, essentially, that she would pay after things settled down. There were dozens of signatures on the front and back of the sheet of paper.

I had a feeling that a blank sheet of paper was soon going to be worth more than one printed with a picture of Ronald Reagan in a cowboy hat.

Roz got into line, and we settled in for a leisurely lunch of crunchy chow mein. There was no way to boil water without breaking up furniture for a fire, and the food wouldn't completely soften with cold water. But if you didn't know where it came from, you might take it for some new exotic oriental dish.

There was a kind of flea market set up on the lawn outside the hospital, three folding tables covered with things of some or no value. An exquisite pearl-and-diamond necklace next to an almost-full box of .22 ammunition; the ammo worth more than the jewelry.

Elza traded a good Eterna writing stick for an odd kitchen implement—three small hourglasses mounted together, timing out three, four, and five minutes. A useful timepiece for standing guard watches.

After about an hour, the nurse came back and collected Elza; they were seeing patients in order of the severity of their problems. When she returned she was wearing a clear plastic cast and a dazed expression, still buzzing with painkillers. She claimed she was ready to move on, but agreed to rest in the shade until her eyes uncrossed.

They put on a stretchy sling that held Dustin's left arm against his chest, and went under the other arm in a kind of figure eight. It reduced the pain from the broken collarbone but restricted his movements. Roz's rib wasn't broken, just a big bruise, and I was only worth a few dabs of antiseptic and plastiflesh. Felt funny on the inside of my lips.

If I'd been sitting two rows back, the tree that killed Stack would've hit me. Mother always said I was born lucky.

We still had a few hours of light, so chose not to spend the night in Holstock. There were plenty of empty houses, and no reason not to commandeer one, except that word would get around. Our weapons and ammunition were our only defense, but they were also a concentration of the only kind of wealth that had meaning in some circles.

We got all our gear together and started off going north on 2031, keeping an eye out for the gravel "fire road" that Mr. Lerner had described. It would only be a few miles, and Paul and Namir agreed that it would be better to spend the night on guard hidden out in the woods, as we had night before last, than be exposed on the side of the abandoned autoway.

I wasn't so sure. Nobody could sneak up on us if we were out in the open. Of course, my judgment might have been affected by fatigue. I was tired of playing soldier and water boy. I wanted to find a piece of shade and collapse into it.

It was only about an hour, though, before we found the gravel road that plunged into the forest to the left. We followed it for a few hundred yards uphill and made camp before it started to go downhill again.

We settled in for the night in a little clearing that wasn't visible from the fire road, leaving one person on guard by the road.

I had the fourth watch, roughly two till four. Staying awake was no trouble; some animal kept moving around somewhere out of sight.

Elza's timer was easy to see in the moonglow. I counted out twenty-four five-minute turns and went to wake Dustin. The creature had stopped making noise, so I slept easily on my bed of fragrant branches, next to Paul but not touching. I could have used some contact, but he was sleeping soundly.

I woke to an unpleasant surprise: we had company. Spy, squatting at the base of a tree like an unholy white Buddha. His clothing was seamless, as if he had been dipped in plastic.

Elza had stood the last watch. She didn't know when he had appeared; hadn't said anything to him.

He stared at me with silent intensity. "So how long have you been here?"

"What makes you think I ever left?" He stood and brushed himself off. "The Others asked me to show myself."

"Why?"

"They don't explain why they do things. Maybe they wanted to introduce an irritant."

Paul came up beside me. "Jesus. And no coffee."

"Here." Spy made a small motion with one hand, and two white china mugs appeared at our feet, steaming, aromatic.

Paul picked one up. "This isn't real."

"Try it."

The mug was solid, hot. The coffee tasted good.

"I know it looks and feels real."

A cup appeared in Spy's hand and he sipped. "But you can't make something out of nothing?"

"That's part of it."

"Do you know the story about the primitive savages who were shown their first movie? Twentieth century, film image projected on a screen."

"Enlighten me."

"They looked behind the screen, and there was nothing there. Subsequently, the image disappeared to them. Because it wasn't real."

"Is that true?" I said.

He smiled. "I read it in a book."

I heard Roz come up behind me.

"Hello," she said. "What the hell are you?"

"Hello, Roz. Think of me as a translator between you and the Others. We decided to call me Spy."

"So what is your real name?"

"I don't need a name. There's only one of me."

She sighed. "Is that coffee?"

❉

Spy eventually conjured a cup of coffee for everyone who wanted it, and afterward sent all the cups back to wherever they'd come from. We had to come up with our own breakfast, though, adding water to boxes of scrambled eggs and refried beans. They heated up nicely but tasted a little plastic.

"It would be a friendly gesture," Namir said to Spy, "if you agreed not to travel with us."

"Wouldn't it?" Spy agreed. "But I have my orders, so to speak."

Paul pointed the riot gun in his direction. "I could blow you to pieces, and then chop up the pieces with the machete. But I guess that would be a waste of ammunition."

"I don't know. You're welcome to try."

He looked like he was considering it. "I wouldn't give you the satisfaction."

It was a storybook-beautiful morning, walking through the waking forest, but the gravel was starting to bother my feet. Get some sturdy walking shoes the next time we came to a store.

Spy walked in front with Paul, who didn't say anything to him. I went up the line to ask Paul a question, but forgot it instantly. Three men stepped out of hiding with guns leveled. "Drop it!" one said to Namir, and then pointed his gun at me.

Paul carefully set down his weapon, and I did the same. I remembered him clipping a holster with one of the pistols under his shirt at the small of his back, but didn't know whether it was still there. Everybody else put their guns down.

Two of the men were stocky and one slim, all of them white and shirtless, with identical Toyota tattoos on their chests. Their weapons were civilian, obviously expensive, more wood than metal, elaborately carved.

"Saw you on the cube, asshole," the bigger one said. I braced myself, but he was talking to Spy. "You're the mouthpiece for the aliens."

"I am their avatar," he said neutrally.

"I'll give you a message." He aimed the rifle at Spy's chest and fired a burst of three or four shots at him.

He rocked back at the impact. But there was no blood, not a mark on him where the bullets had struck. "You missed," he said.

He hadn't, of course, but he stepped closer and fired four measured shots point-blank. Spy simply absorbed them.

"Hold it, Number One," the slender one said. He shrugged out of the pack he was carrying and unsnapped a wicked-looking axe from it. "Let's see you disappear *this*." He hefted it with one hand and stepped forward to swing.

"Could work," Spy said, and pointed a finger at him. There was a pop noise like a toy gun, and the top part of the man's head, above the eyebrows, blew off. His determined expression didn't change as he fell dead.

"Shit," the leader said, and stepped back. Spy pointed the finger at him, and said "bang." A stream of bullets chewed a hole out of the center of his chest. Daylight showed through before he fell.

The third one threw down his gun and ran back into the woods.

Namir picked up one of the weapons and inspected it, avoiding the bloody stock. It hinged open in the middle.

"Sportsmen," he said, and shook one cartridge out. "One powder bullet, but if you miss, you can fry the beast with a laser."

"One shot would be plenty," Paul said, looking at the huge cartridge. "I don't guess we need it, though."

"Carry them a while and throw them away," Namir said. "Throw the bullets away someplace else." He slung the man's assault rifle over his shoulder and looked around the bloody scene. "I suggest we not waste time burying this . . . human waste."

"In the old days," Roz said, "they'd hang them from the trees as a warning."

"This will do," Paul said. "Let's move on."

"I'll search them first," Namir said. He and Dustin started going through pockets. I gave the spray of blood and brains a wide berth, but did look through the skinny one's pack. Half a loaf of hard bread and four tins of sardines. A plastic bag had three rounds for the big-game rifle and a handful of smaller cartridges.

There was an envelope with three detailed maps, one of them the whole state of California. A wallet full of useless money and a roll of California hundred-dollar bills, held together with a rubber band. A metal flask full of liquor.

One side pocket had a small silver pistol, and another held two boxes of ammunition for it, .25 caliber. Paul suggested I keep them, though they wouldn't be much use in a "real" fight. I might get into an unreal one, I supposed.

He offered me a hand grenade with only a little blood on it. I demurred, and Roz stuck it in her purse.

The pack had plenty of room for the encyclopedia volumes and food I was carrying in the cloth bag. It only had two specks of blood, but did give me an uncomfortable, unclean feeling as I hoisted it onto my back and tightened the straps. A dead man's chest, complete with a bottle of rum. But it was easier than carrying the heavy cloth bag. Paul snapped the small axe onto the side.

In case the noise of the encounter might have attracted unwelcome attention, Namir set us up hiding along the bluff that overlooked the road, to watch and wait for an hour. So I took the pack off again after wearing it for a few seconds.

Some kind of birds clattered down behind us to feed on the dead. They didn't caw or cackle; there was no noise but the thud of their beaks and the tearing of cloth and flesh.

They were still playing with their food when Namir finally declared an hour had passed, and we set off into the still-cool morning.

We used the same pattern as the previous day, with an added precaution: whenever we stopped to rest, Dustin would sneak back to make sure we weren't being followed.

People who would follow after what we left behind would be made of sturdy stuff. I got a glimpse of the buzzards' banquet hall, ribs glistening out of two piles of red guts. The ripped remains of a face.

Though I supposed scenes like that would become common as sunsets in most the world. How many billion were left today? Five? With how many months of food? Four?

It was high noon by the time we reached the autoway. There was a tall fence topped with barbed wire, but the bottom of it had been burned open with a laser, the edges of the hole rounded beads of melt.

We went back to the shade of the forest to eat and have an hour of rest.

Spy was studying a web woven densely in the lower branches of a shrub.

"Looks like a caterpillar," I said.

"*Malacosoma californicum.* Happily unaware of everything,"

"Is it going to die soon?"

"They don't live very long." He picked up a stick and gently probed the web.

"I mean 'are the Others going to kill it, along with us and everything else?'"

He didn't look at me. "I really don't have the faintest idea. They don't consult me. Though presumably they know what I'm doing and thinking."

"What do you *think*, then? Is there any chance we'll get our world back?"

"If I were a human," he said to the web, "and thought like a human, I would ask myself how on Earth the Others might benefit from restoring my world. What answer would I come up with, thinking as a human?"

"But you aren't a human," I insisted. "What do *you* think?"

He did look at me, with eyes as realistic and expressionless as a department store dummy's. "In so many ways, that is not a meaningful question. There is no *me* here to think with. You should know that by now."

"When you killed the man who was coming at you with an axe—"

"It was like swatting a fly. His partner was another annoyance. The one who ran away was of no concern. I knew that his testimony would spare us further interruptions."

As he said that, we had an interruption, not particularly dramatic. A girl of about twelve came through the fence hole, chattering in Spanish, crying. Namir talked to her for a minute, calming her down.

"Her parents had a general store north of here. They've disappeared, and the store was gutted by looters. She waited for two days, and when her parents didn't come home, she set out looking for them."

She wailed something and sat down on the ground, wiping her eyes.

"She's afraid they're dead," he said. "I don't know what to say to her."

Tell her she's right? Roz came over and spoke to her softly in halting Spanish.

"Her name's Hermosa, and she has relatives in San Sebastian, the way we're headed, maybe ten miles down the road. Take her there?"

"Sure," Namir said. "How much can she eat in ten miles?"

Quite a lot, as it turned out; a growing girl who'd been hungry for a couple of days. She hadn't made any preparation for travel—just fled when she heard voices in the middle of the night. She said she had hidden from roving gangs as big as a hundred people. Even allowing for a twelve-year-old's imagination, we had better be prepared.

Paul and I would "guard" Spy and Hermosa—stay out of trouble, that is, being the ones least experienced with weapons and mayhem. Namir and Elza would sneak forward a half mile or so, and come back to get us if the coast was clear. Roz and Dustin would stay behind, hidden, long enough to make sure we weren't being followed. So we moved like a sort of elastic inchworm, with four legs in front and four behind. Paul and I and the two supernumeraries bulging along in the belly of the beast.

Hermosa asked Spy one question, and he answered in crisp, rapid Spanish. She quieted and moved to put me and Paul between herself and him.

"What did you just say?" I asked.

"She asked if I was a monster from space. I told her that all three of us were from space, and which of us were monsters depended on who you asked. Fair enough?"

"She seems to have figured it out," Paul said, patting her on the shoulder. "Though actually, you've been more like an ally today. I don't know what those clowns might've done to us."

"That was fortunate for you," he agreed. "I think it would have been a gun battle at close quarters. Many of you would have been hurt, perhaps killed."

"The timing of your appearance was propitious."

"As it often is. Would you care to commit a logical fallacy now?"

Paul frowned at him. *"Post hoc, ergo propter hoc,"* I said, since Dustin wasn't around to say it. "Just because B follows A, it doesn't mean that A caused B."

"Yeah, I got it. Don't worry; I didn't think you conjured up those gangers. If you or the Others wanted to threaten us, you could do it more directly."

"But would we? Just to play the devil's advocate. Maybe I want you to trust me, and so manufactured an incident that would inspire trust."

"And then throw in a counter-argument," I said, "just to keep us confused."

"I like this game," he said.

After a few minutes of silence, Paul said, "Why don't bullets affect you? I mean, they *do* have some effect; I've seen you rock back when they hit you. But then, nothing happens."

"Well, something does happen. I feel them touch and, as you say, I apparently absorb some of their momentum. Then I absorb the metal itself."

"It doesn't hurt?" I asked.

"There's some sensation. More like pleasure than pain, I think.

"I know it takes a lot of energy, or something like energy, to put me here and keep me here. I 'absorb' the kinetic energy of bullets and the chemical energy of food and the radiant energy from sunlight, and it all helps keep me here."

"So if we locked you up in a light-tight box and didn't feed you, you'd disappear?"

"You're welcome to try. I think I'd just reappear outside, though. Or eat the box."

Paul nodded, thoughtful. "Are you invulnerable, then?"

"I don't think so. There must be limits. I could stand inside a burning house, for instance, but couldn't maintain integrity inside a star. I've never tried it, but can't imagine what could manufacture that kind of binding force."

"Likewise a nuke."

"Probably. But I think it would be a waste of time. The Others would just make another one of me."

"I don't suppose a hellbomb would do much," I said.

"A constant blast of radiation? I'd love it! A banquet." He looked up at the sky. "I can feel a little secondary warmth reflected off the atmosphere, from the one you flew over yesterday."

"So radiation and bullets don't bother you," Paul said, "but you protected yourself from an axe."

"That might've hurt. At any rate, it would have taken me time to rebuild, and during that time there would have been trouble."

We walked along in silence for a bit, Paul frowning. "So whose side are you on, anyhow?"

He pointed a thumb at Paul's assault rifle. "Whose side is that gun on?"

"It's on the side of the person who owns it."

"Really?" He reached over carefully and rubbed dirt from the rear end of the barrel, then scratched it with a thumbnail. He peered at what it revealed.

"According to the serial number, it's an actual antique. In another year, it will be a hundred years old.

"It was manufactured in Argentina, for the Paraguayan armed forces, who at the time were fighting Uruguay and Cuba."

"Cuba wasn't a state anymore?" I said.

"Temporarily not. But you don't own it, Paul, not really. I think it's actually on the side of the person who pulls the trigger."

"Okay. Splitting hairs."

"You were asking whose side I am on. That weapon is obviously not on the side of Argentina or Paraguay or Uruguay or Cuba, even though people who identify with those places may have 'owned' it. Is it on your side now?"

"It's an inanimate object."

"That's not exactly the answer. When that fellow with the Toyota tattoo stepped out of hiding and ordered you to drop this gun, why didn't you shoot him?"

"That's obvious."

"He and the other two would have killed you. Because of the gun. Whose side would it be on, then?"

"That's pretty tortuous."

"Not really; not at all. You're asking whose side I'm on. What if you ask me to do something that I know will result in your death? Or Carmen's, or the whole group's, or the country's or the planet's or the solar system's?"

"Okay. So I ask you and you do it and trillions of people die. So it's my fault?"

"Billions. But who said anything about 'fault'? You asked whose side I am on. By all evidence, Paul, I'm on your side."

"I'm honored, especially if you would murder billions of people on my behalf. But you're manifestly not on my side. You're on the side of the Others."

"I'm not sure that's true. I'm not sure it has any meaning. The Others don't use tools, including organisms like you and me, the same way that humans do. To solve problems, to answer questions. That's how different they are. As far as I can tell, they're totally incurious."

"I guess we would be, too," I said, "if we already knew everything and could do anything."

"They obviously fall short of that," Paul said, "or we wouldn't be fighting. They'd just crush us and move on."

Spy nodded. "That's part of the mystery. You might not have anything they need, or at least they've never taken anything from you."

"A *moon*," Paul said. "Jesus Christ, Spy!"

"They destroyed it, as they did Triton. But that's not *taking*.

"They did make a tool out of the moon, so to speak—broke it up into rocks and gravel to surround the Earth with junk, to keep humans from leaving the planet."

"Which worked so well," I said.

"For two weeks," he said. "That's something I may not understand about them. Can they have been surprised that humans reacted by trying to get into space anyhow?"

"You wouldn't be? Surprised."

"Of course not. But it's not as if they said 'If you try to get into space, we'll turn off the electricity.' They presented you with a problem, and it's human nature to step up and try to solve it."

"Wait. Are you making excuses for us?"

"No; just trying to understand *them*. If I know that much about human nature, they must as well. So what's the point in punishing you for being true to your nature?"

"Training us," Paul said, "like some Old Testament God."

"Not exactly. That God would say 'Don't look back at the city' before he turned you into a pillar of salt. The difference isn't subtle."

"This god is an all-powerful infant," I said, "throwing tantrums that blow up worlds. Kill millions. We should be training *it*."

Spy gave me a strange look. "Maybe you are."

# 14

Everybody was dead tired when we came to an overpass and Paul suggested we take one short break, out of the afternoon sun, and then press on till dark. We flopped down and I heard Paul and Namir agreeing that we shouldn't take the state road that passed overhead. It followed a winding route to the sea in one direction and back to Oregon in the other.

Spy began to squat in his Buddha style, but then stood up straight. "Trouble," he said, and disappeared with a pop.

"Hey, come back," Roz said. My sentiment, too.

"Lock and load everything," Namir said. I jacked a round into the chamber of my assault rifle and took the little pistol from my knapsack, cocked it, and stuck it in my belt. My hands started to shake, and I couldn't catch my breath.

"Roz," he said, "tell Hermosa to climb up to the road overhead and hide."

"Might be too steep," she said. I'd never make it myself. Not even when I was twelve. The little girl obediently scrambled up, but slid back.

She didn't have time for a second try. There was a soft whirring sound, and from around the curve a line of black-clad men on bicycles rolled toward us. One in the middle blew a whistle, and they slowed to a stop, staying in line.

There were nine of them. Three had new-looking bikes with luminous CA HIWAY PATROL shields in front. The other six bikes looked random and stolen.

They all seemed to have pistols, and two of the three official bikes had rifle scabbards. They got off the bikes almost in unison and stood by them. The one with a silver whistle on a chain had a large automatic weapon in an awkward-looking holster. He left his bike parked and stepped forward with his hand on the butt of the weapon. "We're the California—"

"We don't care," Namir snapped. "You have no authority over us, and we have you outgunned. Just pedal on, and there won't be any trouble." I'd never heard him use that tone before. Very military and alpha-male.

Even with Namir's weapon pointed toward him, the leader stood his ground. "You don't want to do this. You couldn't take on nine men with body armor, even if you *did* have more guns."

Namir raised his weapon higher and pointed it at the man's face. "Turn around and go."

"*No son policía,*" Hermosa said in a squeaky voice, and pointed past the leader. She said a couple of names.

I'm not sure quite what happened then, and in what order. One or two of them fired, and both Hermosa and Roz crumpled. The leader had his gun out of the holster and fired, I think into the ground, as a blast from Namir's weapon tore half his head off. His helmet spun away, and before it hit the ground everyone was shooting.

I had the pistol out and held it the way they'd shown me, both hands, but I wasn't aiming, just pulling the trigger as fast as I could, pointing at the black-clad men, most of whom had dived to the ground and were firing from a prone position. When the pistol was empty, I threw it down and raised the rifle.

Sharp sting in my left thigh and I fell down backwards, rifle clattering away. I curled into a ball, clutching the wound. There was a lot of blood, and I was peeing, too. I might have been screaming, but all I remember is gunfire and then a big explosion, and silence.

Roz was still alive, though she had a long wide wound to her face; she'd managed to dig that hand grenade out of her bag and throw it at the bikes.

Only one of the enemy was still standing, staggering, and Namir cut him down when he raised his rifle to aim. Or perhaps to surrender. The others were lying on the ground, still or writhing in pain. With her good arm, Elza took a pistol from the closest dead one and walked among them, shooting each one once in the head. The expression on her face was stony and terrible.

I kicked off my sandals and pulled down my pants, already sodden with blood. Blood from the wound was flowing freely but not spurting. The bullet had missed my vagina by two finger widths. A shallow rip about three inches long.

"Put this on it." Dustin was holding out a thick white bandage with ribbons hanging from four corners. I pressed it to the wound while he laced the ribbons around and tied them tight. I should have made some sexual joke but was busy trying to keep my lunch down. He pressed an ampoule into my thigh below the wound.

"Okay. Lie back and rest, try to rest."

"Where's Paul?" I was starting to drift.

He shook his head. "Don't know." I got up on one elbow but it gave way. Dustin eased me back, and I blacked out.

❁

When I woke it was cooler and growing dark. Elza was smoothing a patch onto the back of my hand, some sort of quick stim. Blood pounded in my ears, and I saw sparkles flare and dim.

"We have to move," she said. "I'd like to let you sleep."

"Paul?" I said.

She chewed her lower lip. "He's alive, Carmen. Just."

I felt light; insubstantial, like zero gee. Maybe like a ghost. I stood up and fought dizziness. I could feel stitches pulling on the wound in my thigh, and the grip of fleshtape, but it didn't hurt. Just cold underneath the skin.

Elza stroked the back of my head, patting my short hair. It had grown out enough to make me look like a boy instead of a baldie. When had I last looked in a mirror?

There was a pile of black-clad bodies and a small grave. A shovel was stuck in the soft dirt. Waiting?

Dustin sat with crossed legs next to Paul, who was stretched out on a sheet of dark plastic lettered CALIFORNIA HIGHWAY PATROL. When I got closer I saw that the plastic was really light green. The darkness was blood, dried or clotting.

Paul was shirtless, a thick wad of bandage taped over his chest, and his right hand was hidden inside another blood-soaked wad. Forehead wrapped in fresh white gauze.

Only the whites of his eyes showed. His breathing was a quiet, labored rasp.

Namir came up beside me and stood close, not touching. "It's a wonder he's alive," he whispered. "A bullet went completely through his chest and out the back."

"The head wound?" I said, feeling horribly detached. The man I love is dying?

"Might be a skull fracture." I couldn't ask about the hand.

"Shall I try to wake him up?" Elza said.

"Let him rest," I said. "If he's going to die, let him go." Words I didn't want to say but couldn't take back.

"We have to get out of the open," Namir said. "Roz found a place a couple of hundred meters down the road."

I looked around. Not a good place to spend the night, the road in a tight loop. People could sneak up from both sides and overhead.

The sun was setting in a brilliant swirl of scarlet and orange and purple. "Could I be with him for just a minute? Alone with him."

The three of them moved quietly away. I heard someone gathering hardware.

The skin of his face was cold and wet, but his forehead was warm. I touched his eyelids but got no reaction. They stayed closed.

He made a noise in his throat, like an "R." My name? I said his name, and he took a breath and made the sound again. He opened one eye and tipped his head slightly toward me. "Arm," he whispered. "Be?"

That was a lot better than nothing. "You'll be all right," I said, with more conviction than I felt. "We have to move you. Get out of the open."

He nodded slightly and closed his eyes.

Namir and Dustin helped me carry him, using the plastic sheet as a floppy stretcher. We had to rest twice, but managed to haul him up the road and over a concrete berm, to where Elza was standing guard. Roz was asleep in the weedy grass, and didn't wake up when we settled Paul next to her.

"Check your leg," Dustin said. I took off my trousers, and he and Elza studied my crotch more carefully than anyone had done in a while.

"Not my best work," Elza said, carefully tracing the line of the stitches. She licked her thumb and rubbed dried blood away. It was still numb. "Might have to be redone by a real doctor someday." If someday ever comes.

The stim still had me tingling, though from the heaviness in my arms and legs I knew I was headed for a crash landing when it wore off. So Elza let me take over for the first guard watch, while I was still wide-eyed.

As soon as it was fully dark, I could hear scavengers of some kind down by the pile of bodies. I hoped all the fresh meat lying around would keep them from digging up the grave.

But did it really make any difference? Wolves above the ground or worms below. I tried to get that out of my mind.

That poor little girl, who came to us for protection. Welcome to the Carmen Dula good-luck streak. What had Card said? *Maybe it wasn't Mars ... maybe you're to blame for the whole fucking shooting match.* Though it was starting to feel more like a shooting gallery than a match, the targets falling two by two.

My raw right hand still felt the pumping recoil of the pistol; the web of my thumb was skinned where the slide had rubbed over it.

I heard claws rattle on the pavement below me, then stop. A dog or a wolf was looking up at me in the darkness. I pushed the safety knob forward, and after that quiet click the claws moved on.

They knew we were here. But they weren't hungry. Not yet.

Namir relieved me at ten o'clock. Paul was conscious and talking quietly, breathing without trouble. I slept straight through till Roz woke me at six. Like good little soldiers, we cleaned and inspected our weapons. Check the action but don't carry a round in the chamber. Irrelevant to Namir himself, with his double-barreled shotgun always ready.

(When the bikers attacked, I hadn't gone for my own assault rifle, strapped across my back. I had the pistol in my hand and just emptied it, and then stood there like a target while I fumbled with the rifle. The bullet that hit me might have saved my life, since it put me flat on the ground before Roz's grenade went off. All the shrapnel went over my head.)

We dined on crunchy dried rations. There was a temporary toilet-paper crisis, solved by Ronald Reagan.

"Another perfect day in paradise," Paul groaned when he woke, blinking up at the unbroken blue sky. "Have we decided who's going, who's staying?"

"Only Roz and I are comfortable with horses," Namir said. Someone had to fetch a horse and cart from Funny Farm, to carry Paul.

"I guess you ought to go," Paul said. "Dustin and the girls can protect me."

"Girls," I said. "We'll bake him some fucking cookies."

"Leave this with you," Namir said, setting the riot gun down next to him. He rattled the box of shells. "Don't spend them all in one place."

Elza had the light machine gun and two short belts of ammunition. She held up a belt, and he shook his head, no. "Just a pistol. I'm not getting into any gun battles." He hoped.

He looked at the sun. "Eight hours there, maybe three back, depending on the horse situation."

"And whether you get lost," Roz said. Without a native guide.

"Straightforward enough. I'll stay close to the road."

"Stop if it gets dark," I said, unnecessarily.

"Be back before that," he said without conviction. He pulled his rucksack straps tight and squeezed my arm. "Take care."

He turned into the woods and disappeared.

We decided to keep the two-hour guard interval, with one of us standing watch at the top of the berm, looking down the road toward the bodies, and another hiding up the road in the other direction.

I did that one first, lying behind some thick brush that gave me a clear line of sight down to the road. Saw two squirrels and heard others arguing overhead. No birds. I passed the time making letters and even whole words out of the random lines presented by the clutter of stems and branches in front of me. THIT THIT, one area lisped, and I could but agree.

Roz eventually came to relieve me, her face looking a little better. She'd taken off the emergency fleshtape and cleaned the line of stitches and then re-applied new fleshtape more evenly. Still a bad rip from eye to chin, and she had to drink through a straw. She offered her thermos to me, a harsh mixture of tepid instant coffee and rum. Not my usual before-lunch pick-me-up, but memorable.

Dustin was stretched out on top of the berm, looking down over the machine-gun sights at the pile of bodies, which was not as orderly as it had been. When I got up to where he was, I could smell them, a slight whiff of rot.

"Wait till they've been in the sun all day," he said. He handed me the hourglass contraption and adjusted the figure-eight sling, grimacing.

"Any of those wolves?"

"Dogs, I think, but no. Not since it got light." He put his hand lightly on top of the gun. "I guess Namir told you, it's a hair trigger. Just tap it and get off, that'll be two or three shots."

I looked at the two belts beside it. "And we only have, what, fifty?"

"Actually forty-eight. You could burn it all up in a few seconds."

"I'll be careful." Namir had emphasized that it was mainly a psychological weapon, to make us seem more powerful than we were. "It's cocked?"

"Ready to go. Don't touch it till you can see the whites of their eyes." I think that was some kind of a joke. But how close would that be? Besides, it's California; the natives all wear sunglasses.

Maybe I would fire when they were close enough to hit.

I wondered whether I had killed anyone yesterday, blasting away at random. If it was important, I could go down and look at all the bodies. See if anyone had been felled by a single tiny shot.

That was a topic that had come up now and then on the starship. Namir was obviously bothered by it, having killed a carload of people as a young soldier, and more than a dozen more later in life. (He had never told me this, but had admitted it to Elza one drunken night. It was not official spy business for Mossad, but personal revenge just after Gehenna. In one day, he tracked down and killed eleven enemies with bare hands or a knife, and six more later.)

None of the rest of us had had anything like that experience, though Elza and Dustin were supposedly skilled in the art and craft of murder, and Paul had gone through basic training, and learned about bayonets and hand-to-hand fighting and all. Namir said a single killing changed you forever, separated you from the rest of the human race with a silent barrier. One time he wondered whether it was like motherhood—an experience that was common and yet so profound that having it or not divided the race into two species.

Our philosopher Dustin pointed out that both actions gave humans powers that normally are reserved for gods: giving life and taking it.

So was I a god yet? Or did it only count if you were sure you had done it, and what if you thought you had done it but hadn't? At least that didn't happen in childbirth. Did I leave a baby around here somewhere? Well, my own status as a mother was problematic.

The carrion birds who were feeding on the pile took off with a confused clash of heavy wings. I didn't see anything. My finger moved closer to the hair trigger as I willed myself not to touch it, not yet.

Then I was touching. Just enough to feel the cold of it. I shifted slightly, so the barrel was lined up with the darkness under the underpass.

The shadow moved and a shape inched into the sun. Not a wolf, too big.

A bear, its brown fur coppery in the sun. It looked left and right, then waddled directly toward the pile of bodies. Then it—she—looked back toward the shadow, and two cubs came out in a line.

Feeding time at the zoo. She went to a body that was lying separate from the others, and flipped it over with one pat. It didn't have much of a face, and its belly was open, guts trailing. She tore at the clothes and got the pants halfway down and ripped away at the meat. She ate a little, but mainly seemed to be flensing it for the cubs, pulling out strips of gray-and-red flesh. There wasn't as much blood as you would expect.

The cubs rolled around, playing with their lunch, and would have been cute in another context. The mother left them, stepped up to the top of the pile of bodies, and looked around.

She looked straight at me.

I couldn't breathe. Should I just shoot? How fast can a bear charge?

She growled, loud and scary, and shook her huge head, and turned to look at the cubs.

I heard someone creeping up behind me. If it was another bear, it was a little one.

"What the fuck?" Dustin whispered, philosophically. "Are there bears here?"

"Three, anyhow. You left Paul?"

"He's awake. Has the riot gun." He set his own rifle down silently, parallel to mine, and crouched low. "I don't suppose they're going anywhere soon."

"Not unless something bigger comes along."

His gun was a fancy sporting model with a big telescopic sight. He peered through it and clicked something twice, not electronic.

"Don't shoot."

"Won't unless we have to. Try a head shot if we do."

"Probably bounce off." As if to demonstrate something, she closed her jaws around a body's head, evidently trying to crack the skull. But he was wearing a hard plastic bike helmet, and she tossed him away. The next one cracked like a walnut.

"I guess we're safe as long as she has all that food," Dustin said, still peering through the sight.

I wasn't so sure. "They're predators, not scavengers. If she knew we were up here, she might attack."

"Would she?"

"How the hell should I know? We didn't have bears on Mars."

"Didn't used to have them here. Except on the flag."

"What?" Stars and stripes and a bear?

"California state flag. I guess they were here in the old days."

I had a chill. "Namir will be coming back this way, with the horse. He'll be using the road."

"That's some time from now. Maybe they'll eat their fill and move on."

"Why should they?" How fastidious could they be? Momma, this one tastes bad. Shut up and clean your plate.

I shifted my weight and was rewarded with a sharp stab of pain in my thigh.

"What?"

"Painkiller's wearing off. My leg."

"Kit's down by Paul. I'll keep an eye on this."

"Thanks." I tried to inch away silently, but the underbrush made little scraping noises. When I was far enough down the berm, I stood up slowly. Dustin looked back and nodded.

My head spun and I lurched, limping, down to the first-aid kit. Paul had rolled onto one elbow, holding the shotgun up at an angle. He waved a salute. "What's the commotion?"

"Bears down on the road. You're feeling better?"

"Weak. Couldn't outrun a bear."

"Me, neither." I found the box of Anodyne ampoules and read the instructions. Not more than two in one twenty-four-hour period. Unless you're in a plane wreck and get shot by bicycle gangers. Then you can take all you want.

I sat down and wriggled out of my pants and popped the ampoule near the wound.

"Could I have some?" Paul said, and for a mad moment I thought he was talking about what I had just exposed.

"When did you last have one?"

He touched the head bandage gingerly. "Guess it's too soon. How's your leg?"

"Good thing I have two." I pulled my pants back up and sat next to him, stroking his arm. "Should you be sitting up?"

"Yeah. Maybe not." He flopped back down. I went over to the pack pile and picked up the extra assault rifle. It already had a round chambered, which would probably get me flogged in Namir's army. Go ahead, I can take it. I get shot in the crotch and come back for more. Chew up the bullets with my—

"Hello, again." Spy had materialized between me and Paul. This time he looked like he'd been dipped in dark green plastic, less conspicuous.

It took me a moment to find my voice. "Are you always going to disappear when we need you most?"

"I have no control over that. As I told you."

"You know what happened while you were gone?"

"Yes. I'm sorry I wasn't here to help. I could have drawn their fire, at least, and returned it, like last time."

"Do you know anything about bears?"

"Of course I do. You don't have to worry about the ones on the road."

"The big one looks pretty formidable."

"Don't worry about her."

There was a sudden blast of gunfire, and I dove to the ground. Then another. It was coming from the berm where I'd just left Dustin.

Spy hadn't moved. "Poor bear."

I staggered back to my feet and limped up the berm, pulse hammering. Stringent powder smell.

Dustin was stretched out prone, rigid, sighting through the rifle-scope. A curl of blue smoke blew away from the muzzle.

The adult bear was lying inert on the slope coming up from the pavement. It had covered about half the distance before it fell.

The two cubs were sitting on the road, looking up at us.

"Don't go down yet," Dustin said without looking up.

"What happened?"

"She heard us or smelled us or something. Charged straight up the hill."

"Spy knew it was going to happen."

"I wasn't surprised, myself." He looked back at me. "What do you mean, 'Spy'?"

He walked up next to me. "Hello, Dustin."

"You just come and go as you please, don't you?"

"No. As I was telling Carmen, I don't have any control over it. I'm here, and then I'm nowhere for an instant, and then I'm back here, with something like a memory of what happened while I was away."

"Not a 'memory,'" I said. "Just 'something like' one."

"Don't I always speak carefully, Carmen? I can't say the word exactly in English, or any other human language, but 'memory' is close."

Dustin stood up with the rifle. "Better go check the bear."

"Don't worry. It's dead."

"You knew that before it happened," I said.

"Not really. I suppose you might say 'premonition.' But really it's no more supernatural than statistics. As we came closer in space-time to the bear's death, it became more and more clear to me that the bear was going to die."

I felt suddenly cold. "You knew back then. You disappeared at the overpass. Just before the gangers killed the little girl."

"I did not know. Not exactly. Just before I went away, I had a feeling of certainty that death was on its way. Who or when, I didn't know. Then I was gone."

"Where?" Dustin said.

"I don't know; everything goes dark for a while. I assume it's like sleeping is for humans. But I've never slept."

"You had this feeling," I said, "but you didn't say anything to us about it."

"He did, though," Dustin said. "You told us to watch out or something."

"I said 'trouble.' Then everything went black. That's when I disappeared, to you."

"Like the Others wanted to get you out of harm's way," I said.

"That's not it." He gave me a peculiar searching look. "They don't care any more about me than they do about you. Maybe less; if they lose me, they can make a new one."

"Did you have a premonition back then?" Dustin said. "Like, 'watch out; there's a bunch of gangers on bikes headed this way'?"

"Not that specific. I did know . . . what I was about to say . . . was that danger was coming; death was coming. I knew it was an outside agency."

"But the Others snatched you away before you could warn us," I said.

"He did start to."

"I wonder," Spy said. "Another few seconds, and I might have realized we had to get off the road. We might have escaped their notice."

He raised both hands in a human gesture, frustration or helplessness. "There are things I can't know about the Others. It's like . . . as if you made a human avatar, a robot, and gave it no sense of smell or taste . . . and then wired it so it couldn't use the future tense, the subjunctive mood. That's how handicapped I am, from their point of view. As if I knew that smell and taste existed, but had no experience of them and no vocabulary to describe them."

"And the future-tense thing?" Dustin said.

"It's not that they *know* the future, one hundred percent. But nothing ever surprises them, no matter how unlikely."

"And you're sort of like that," I said.

He shrugged. "More so than you."

"So what about tomorrow?" Dustin said. "We'll make it to the farm?"

He shook his head and looked down the slope. The cubs were poking at their mother, trying to rouse her.

"I don't know. I didn't know there would be bears."

# 15

Namir didn't come back before nightfall. We stayed clustered around Paul, at least one of us awake and on guard, on ninety-minute shifts. I hoped the others slept better than I did.

The cubs had left their mother's body before dark. Where did they go? Would they lead other bears back?

The woods were full of small noises. I guess they always are if you're listening.

Spy disappeared sometime around three or four, while I was sleeping. Elza said nothing special happened; she just noticed he was gone.

We all got cold. When the sky started to lighten, we built a small fire, twigs, to thaw out our hands and feet. We warmed some water in a metal cup and shared bad instant coffee.

An hour or so after dawn, Namir showed up, riding a horse and leading a mule with a cart. He brought a bag of hard-cooked eggs and a bottle of wine. We attacked the eggs but left the wine for later.

Namir took a piece of paper from his shirt pocket and unfolded it carefully. It had been handled quite a bit. "That fellow with the telescope, Wham-O. He saw something on Mars, and made a drawing."

It was a smudged pencil sketch, clear enough.

"That's Syrtis Major," I said, pointing to a shape like a child's drawing of Africa on an Earth globe. "But what's that?

Off the southern tip of the mass was a circle surrounding a cross. Paul's eyes were open, and I showed it to him. "What do you think?"

He squinted at it. "Earth."

"No," I said. "It's Mars."

"The circle with the cross. That means Earth."

"Of course," Namir said. "The astronomer's symbol. Could they have drawn that in the desert sand?"

"Walking in a big circle?" Elza said.

"Not walking," Paul said. "Take heavy equipment. Hundreds of miles."

"Or the Others might have done it," Namir said. "Not a very big project, compared to blowing up the Moon."

"But why would they?" I said, which produced a couple of shrugs.

"I think we did it," Paul said, "we Martians. A signal to Earth, saying we're still alive."

"Let's assume that's it," Namir said, smiling. "If the Others wanted to impress us, they'd do something less subtle."

The Farmers had put an old mattress in the cart, and a length of plastic webbing to strap Paul in securely.

He wasn't complaining about pain, but he looked bad. Elza offered him an ampoule, and when he didn't say no, gave it to him in the shoulder. He was asleep by the time we had him secured.

Namir checked the height of the sun; two and a half fists. "We'll make it before dark, no problem. Early afternoon."

I hoped *I* wouldn't be the problem. My leg was supporting my weight all right, and with the cart and mule I didn't have to carry anything but the rifle.

The mule seemed to like me well enough, so I led it, or at least accompanied it, while Namir trotted ahead a couple of hundred yards at a time. Elza followed a ways behind me, and Dustin was the rear guard, hiding in wait a few minutes before following.

We went along the paved road for about two hours, uphill and then down. In a valley—actually a "saddle," I suppose—we turned off at a place marked by a faded orange tape stapled around a tree. It was not so much a trail as a path that had once been mowed. "Bush-hogged" is the verb I remembered from my Florida childhood. I always had the image of a hairy wild pig with tusks, but I suppose a bush-hog was a kind of mowing machine.

My mulish colleague didn't care for the new trail; the cart didn't roll smoothly and tugged and jerked on its harness. After a minute it stopped cold, and whacking its flank just gave me a sore hand.

Namir came back and dismounted. "It didn't like this part coming up." With his belt knife he cut a supple branch from a sapling, and shook it rattling in the mule's face, muttering at it in Hebrew. It grunted and started moving.

He handed the switch to me. "It remembered. How sweet." He remounted the horse in one smooth motion. Riding boots and a holstered pistol. All he needed was a big hat, and maybe a tobacco cigarette.

He was obviously enjoying it. They'd had a couple of horses on his kibbutz, as well as camels. He said as a boy he liked the camels more; they were more like pets, with personality. But he hadn't ridden one in about a hundred years. He'd ridden horses in the States, back when he led the simple life of an Israeli diplomat and spy.

What different paths we had followed, to wind up so closely entwined. Before he went into space he'd had a full career in that cosmopolitan universe, now as dead as Babylon. New York, Washington, Paris, Moscow, Tel Aviv—all dark and cold now, some in ruins. But he'd lived that life.

What goes through his head? In what languages?

He was a UN diplomat when I was a teenager stepping aboard the Space Elevator for what I thought would be a five-year adventure. While he was going around the world learning and doing, I was stuck in a small town in a cave on Mars. Not even a small town. The same 105 people waging eternal war against dust and boredom.

It never occurred to me that one day I would long for boredom. That I would give anything to be back in that cave with those plain, brave people.

Namir is bullet-brave. But he would have done well in Mars, too. The starship we shared didn't have one hundredth the floor space we enjoyed in Mars. But with one exception, we stayed away from each other's throats. I wouldn't have called it courage then.

The mule's name was Jerry. I whispered endearments and scratched his rump with the stick when we had to pick up the pace. Namir's horse waltzed nervously through the underbrush, but Jerry just plodded along, perhaps conserving strength, and kept up well enough.

We stopped before mid-day to rest and eat. Namir emptied all the cartridges out of one magazine, which had fallen into a stream. He cleaned and polished each round before thumbing it back into place.

Thirty rounds. So much of our world was numbers. Five magazines with thirty rounds each. A double-barreled shotgun with nine. I had twenty-seven left for my pistol and two twenty-round clips for the rifle. Two flare pistols. There were seven ampoules left in the first-aid kit, for three people in pain.

My leg was stiffening up, but I could walk. I hoped they had more ampoules back at Funny Farm, but didn't want to ask. As an experiment, I took a stick of pain gum after we ate. It would probably work fine if I'd been shot in the mouth. It made my tongue disappear, but didn't do much for the groin.

After about an hour, we got to the stream that fed the pool behind Funny Farm, but we didn't follow it. It was a couple of miles shorter to cut through the woods, and it was a good thing we went that way. If we'd followed the stream, we might have been too late.

We were a little more than a mile from home when we heard the first crackle of gunfire. It echoed, but there was no mistaking which direction it was coming from.

Namir turned in the saddle and shouted at me: "Stay here with Paul! Get off the trail!" Good idea.

He snapped the shotgun closed. "Wait until the shooting stops," he said. "If we don't, if I don't come back, Elza, you come check."

"Maybe you should wait," Dustin said.

"Yeah, maybe I should." He nudged the horse hard with his heels, and it trotted forward.

"Good luck?" I said. Are soldiers supposed to wish each other luck? The horse was going pretty fast when they disappeared around the bend.

"We should get hidden," Dustin said. He stroked the mule's nose. "You'll be quiet, won't you?" It tilted its head toward him and wisely didn't say anything. Neither did I.

The shooting continued as we worked the cart and mule through the brush. It was sporadic, not the steady firefight roar I remembered from Armstrong and Camp David. Bullets getting rare on both sides.

Jerry had always been whickering and grunting at me, but it was quiet as we struggled up a small hill. Dustin's innate leadership abilities, or perhaps even a mule knows that when people are shooting guns, you don't want to draw attention. When we got to the top of the rise, he put his big head on my shoulder and breathed hard, but otherwise stayed quiet.

"I'll go up on the other side," Dustin said. "Hold fire if I start shooting; I'll try to draw them away." He looked at me. "If you have to leave Paul, do it."

"No," I said.

"They won't hurt him. They need him."

"No. We don't know who 'they' are."

"If it was you in the cart," Elza said, "we'd stay with you. So get the fuck over there and protect us."

He started to say something but turned and went down the slope.

"So are two husbands twice as much trouble," I whispered to her, "or four times?"

"Eight. These two." She looked down at Paul. "Hope he'll be all right."

"Namir, too."

She nodded. "He always comes out on top. 'Always' meaning so far." Surprisingly, she knuckled away a tear. "We're lucky to have them at all."

"Yeah. What a week."

She sat down heavily and looked at her weapon, propping it up on the cast. "Piece of shit," she said neutrally, and pulled the slide back slowly twice, then fast three times. Five cartridges ejected.

The mule stirred restlessly at the sound.

"Maybe you should have swapped," I said. Her gun had jammed during the melee with the cyclists, but I only found out later; she'd cleared it by whacking it with the cast, and emptied the rest of the clip at them. Then picked up a pistol and made sure the enemy were all dead. Meanwhile, I was distracted by trying not to bleed out.

"Yeah, maybe." She picked up the loose rounds and wiped them off with her shirt tail and snicked them back into the magazine. "Devil you know. I was tempted by the fancy ones those bicycle assholes had. But I know this one, and we have ammo—"

In the distance, a sustained hammering of automatic fire. Two thumps that must have been a shotgun. Then rifles and pistols crackling.

"Sounds like he got there," she said.

"Should we . . ."

"Hold our position, yeah." Jerry made a chuckling noise, and I stroked his ears.

It was like overhearing an argument between machines, angry plosives with a whine now and then. A bullet ricocheting from metal? No, I'd heard it in the woods before.

We should've taken the bulletproof vest from the biker leader. It was all covered with blood and brains, though. So it hadn't done *him* much good. But I had to think what an easy target Namir would present, riding slowly on horseback.

At least smart bullets wouldn't work. Though they seemed to have plenty of dumb ones.

It was quiet for a minute, two minutes, three. "Maybe that's it," Elza said.

Whatever "it" was. I looked across the shallow draw and couldn't see Dustin, which I supposed was good. "So we stay here?"

"Yeah. Stay ready." I checked Paul, and there was no change; he'd slept through the excitement. It hadn't been that loud.

I had to press down pretty hard to feel the pulse in his throat, but it was there. It worried me that he didn't respond to the pressure. He was too pale and still. Did we give him too much painkiller? I resisted the impulse to shake him.

Another minute. "Shit," she said quietly. "Something happen."

"Maybe he's safe inside now," I said.

"That or dead. Or maybe he fell back under fire."

My brain wasn't working. "So we should wait to see if he comes back?"

"Maybe. Shit. I have to go."

For an odd second I thought she was talking about a bowel movement. "Tell Dustin."

She didn't have to. He came out of the brush below us. "Let's get up there. Set up a cross-fire." He looked at me with bright intensity. "You stay here with Paul. We'll be back before dark."

"Stay off the road," Elza added helpfully. She shouldered her bag, and they hustled off.

"Good-bye," I said to their backs, and felt a sudden twist of new fear.

They had abandoned me. A rifle and a pistol and a mule versus how many armed lunatics?

Jerry shifted his weight and snuffled. I held the weapon away from him and put my arm around his neck. "You and me, mule," I whispered. The supernumeraries. The expendables?

The aliens, Paul and me. Martian citizens, if born on Earth. Citizens of the galaxy, the title of a movie I saw as a child in Florida, back in the twenty-first century.

When we were chatting with Lanny in the bookstore, he mentioned there had been a strong movement, before the power went out, to reform the calendar. Why mark years from the disputed date of a minor prophet's birth? That "minor" was Lanny's own prejudice showing, of course. One out of three Americans had been practicing Christians when the lights went out.

That was another one of his jokes—if they had practiced a little harder, maybe they would've gotten it right. And all of this wouldn't have happened.

But his point was interesting. Some people wanted to begin the calendar on the day, the moment, humans first stepped onto another world—the moon, back in 1969. We knew when that had happened, down to the nanosecond.

Paul had liked the idea but said it didn't matter which nanosecond you started your calendar on, so long as everybody agreed on which nanosecond it was. He said it would make astronomical calculations easier if you started the calendar at the beginning of a Julian day, which I guess was the number of days since Julius Caesar was born. I remember resisting the impulse to argue that, after all, Caesar was born by Caesarian section, so at what nanosecond was he actually born? When they cut into his poor mother, or when his head came out of the wound, or his feet, or with his first breath, or when they cut the cord? This is science, after all.

My own children had been "born" the instant the mother machine shocked breath into them; their legal birth date was 23 Lowell 28, which translated into sometime in December, 2084, Earth style.

Maybe they should reform Earth's calendar so year zero and day zero were the same as ours, the day humans first stepped onto Mars. Of course, the calendars and clocks would spin crazily out of synchrony after the first moment.

Computers don't care, anyhow. It's only humans who get confused.

Jerry made a protracted intestinal comment, to remind me that humans and computers weren't everything.

So how did Elza and Dustin plan to keep from being shot by the good guys? Would the fact they were shooting at the bad guys protect them?

I tried to visualize the situation. They'd have to approach on this side of the river, east; it was too deep and fast to cross. But they wouldn't just walk up this road alongside the river. Too exposed, even here.

They'd probably loop around farther east, and circle back behind the stockade. The orchard wouldn't afford much cover, which probably meant the enemy wouldn't be there.

Then what? Holler for someone to cover them while they rushed for the back door? If Namir was there, he could identify their voices. "Don't shoot; they're fellow spies from nonexistent governments."

My degree in American Studies was woefully deficient in course work on staying alive at the end of the world. Find good boots. Count your ammo. Try to keep the mule from farting too loud.

I jumped at gunfire, but recognized it: the "burst of three" setting on the standard-issue army rifles that we were carrying. Two bursts on top of each other. Then one more. Then two more.

Didn't mean it was them, of course. But it wasn't the manic rattle we'd heard before. Had they had time to circle around? Depends on how thick the woods were; how cautious they were.

Jerry backed away from the noise. I patted him and told him it was all right. Lying to a mule, how pathetic.

Paul groaned, and I went around to check on him. No change.

I heard a noise, and crouched down behind the wagon. There was something or someone moving in the brush on the other side of the road, back where Dustin had been.

Thumbed the rifle selector straight up to B3, burst, and peered over it to the other side. It sounded like someone walking, not being careful. But then why not walk on the road?

The wagon was too well hidden; I couldn't have seen anyone unless he was wearing bright clothes. Quietly I stepped around past Jerry, pressing his muzzle, and whispering, "Quiet." He nodded, which was strange. I went down into a shallow ditch that would be a streamlet when it rained. I touched the extra magazines in my pockets, talismans, and crept down toward the road the way I'd been taught, the butt of the rifle stock firm under my arm, finger inside the trigger guard but not on the trigger.

The noise to my right grew louder. About halfway to the road I stopped and waited, hunkered behind a thick brown tangle of dead brush.

The noise stopped, too.

There was the slightest rustle, that could have been wind—but there *was* no wind. I swung the rifle in that direction and a wolf's head appeared, or a dog like a German shepherd, teeth bared and ears flattened down. I fired and the burst went low, scattering dirt a couple of feet below the face, which disappeared.

Probably running away, though I couldn't hear anything but cotton stillness and metallic ringing. Ear protectors dangled in a small plastic bag hanging from the rear sight, so you wouldn't forget to use them.

Assuming he was scared away now, but everyone else within a mile knew where I was, I wasted no time getting back to the cart.

The water and supplies and extra weapons were as I'd left them, strapped to the sides. Jerry was restless but quiet. I looked in the wagon at Paul.

His eyes were open.

"Paul?" No reaction.

I touched his skin and it was cool and dry. He didn't blink when I touched his eyes.

I closed them.

# 16

We had talked a couple of times about whether it was better to lose a loved one suddenly, without warning and with no emotional preparation, or go through the agony of watching them slip away slowly.

For yourself you want it to be sudden and unexpected. But perhaps for the ones you love, you want time to say good-bye.

I still had no clear answer. If the biker gang had killed Paul there by the underpass, I wouldn't have had the hours of talking, or trying to talk, while he slipped away. And he would have been spared the agony of a lingering death. Physical and emotional.

I had stopped crying, and started digging, by the time they came back. Cursing the blunt entrenching tool and the coarse network of roots that resisted it. I only had a small hole when Dustin and Elza came up the slope, along with two men from Funny Farm, Wham-

O and one who introduced himself as Judd when he took the entrenching tool from me with quiet insistence.

"I'm sorry," Elza said. "How many years?"

"Actual? I was eighteen when we met and a few weeks older
when we fell in love, or I did. Twenty-one real years?"

"Not enough."

"No." How many would be enough? We had moved back to the
cart, and I stared down at him, at his body. I wanted to touch him,
and I didn't want to.

Judd had followed me up, holding the small shovel like a toy in
his large hand.

"Ma'am, I'll do whatever you say, but wouldn't it be best if we
buried him in the graveyard up at the farm? You're part of the family now."

"Of course," I said, and did a bad imitation of smiling. "I wasn't,
I'm not thinking straight."

The three men had no trouble convincing Jerry to back and fill
and come back down to the path with them. As we made our way
along, they told me what had happened.

The gunfire we'd heard had evidently been in the nature of a
probe: two or three people with automatic weapons staged an attack on the stockade's front entrance. They killed the man who was
standing guard there.

The "farmers" responded with fire from two of the guardhouses
on the corners of the stockade, but worried they might have used up
too much ammunition in a show of force.

When Dustin and Namir came to their aid, giving flanking fire from the east, the attackers withdrew fast, leaving a blood trail but no bodies.

Other than that first casualty, none of the good guys was injured, but it was a prudent assumption that they hadn't seen the end of it. And they wanted us inside the stockade as soon as possible.

I thanked them for coming to our rescue so quickly. Dustin pointed out that it wasn't exactly charity. Out there, I could be captured and held hostage. Even if they weren't smart enough to do that, weapons and ammunition and a vehicle that ran on grass were beyond price.

A phrase with no meaning. When would things have prices again?

It wasn't just Dustin and Namir and Judd in the rescue party. They said that Namir had wanted to come up with the horse, but the farmers already had a squad organized and on alert, which was how they were able to come back so fast. I never saw more than two of them at a time, but there were eleven others along with Judd, moving through the woods alongside of us, ahead and behind.

We moved along at a pretty good rate, and after about twenty minutes turned up into the road that cuts through the wheat field to the stockade. Judd shouted an order and then stayed back in the woods with his scattered squad.

Jerry stopped for a moment when he saw the building, and then all but trotted toward it. The double door swung open, and Namir came out on horseback to meet us.

He looked in the cart and nodded. "I'm sorry."

"Not unexpected," I had to say, but my voice cracked.

He dismounted and walked alongside me. "You were with him," he said.

"Yes and no. I went off to check on a noise—a dog or a wolf. When I came back he was, he was gone."

"Hard on you."

Yes and no, I thought. That chest wound would not have healed without surgery. Even if he had been sheltered and comfortable, he wouldn't have lasted very long. He probably knew that as well as I did. When we could talk, we talked of other things.

Gunfire to our right, two single shots. The horse and mule both realized it was time for speed, and we were hard-pressed to keep up with them on the way to the door. It slammed shut behind me, but they eased it back open a few inches, a guard watching through the crack.

Not a job anyone would want, sniper bait.

The place didn't seem much changed from before except that some people carried weapons. And there were more of them. Judd confirmed that they had taken in a few neighboring families, who brought food and munitions with them.

Did they turn away people who came empty-handed? I could ask later. There were other horses and mules inside the compound, in a corral improvised from scraps of old lumber. A couple of men held it open for the horse and unhitched Jerry. They both went straight for the pile of hay, and I had a sudden vision of how hard that was to come by now. Harvesting under armed guard, quickly. The same with the orchards and other crops, and nobody would be lazily fishing out of the stream. There were chickens underfoot everywhere, which I supposed had been cute for an hour.

When would it be safe to go back to normal living conditions? Would it ever be?

Namir and Dustin and Elza helped me carry our gear to the small cabin we were sharing with two other couples. Then we went to the rear of the place, to the cemetery garden just beyond the back door.

Four living people were keeping guard in foxholes while a burial party of four others worked fast with pick and shovel. A body lay beside them under a dirty sheet stained with new blood. The man who'd been shot at the beginning of the attack I'd heard from back in the woods.

They passed us the pick, and we started breaking ground for Paul's grave. I did a short turn, the pick much more efficient than our entrenching tool, but almost too heavy for me to swing. After a long and heavy day.

When they finished burying the other man, we stopped digging. Roz came out with two women and two children, and they each said some words, the children crying though the women had finished.

I thought I was done with crying, too, but it started again when the four of us carried Paul's body from the cart, using a blanket as a stretcher. We lowered him into the waist-deep hole and took the blanket out; no winding sheets when cloth was getting rare. I used Namir's knife to cut a square of cloth off my shirt, to cover Paul's face before the dirt fell.

I cried then, and so did Dustin and Elza. Perhaps Namir would have if he could. The only humans on this planet who had been to the stars. Come back to Earth to die.

He would not have wanted a prayer any more than I would. But I tried to remember something he had said to me about how marvelously complex man was in spite of his cosmic insignificance. A shifting assemblage of atoms, mostly carbon, hydrogen, and oxygen, come together to "mimic and define" purpose in its beautiful stagger from cradle to grave.

He had been a beautiful man, full of humor and courage and love. I said that, too, after Dustin and Elza gave their farewells, and Namir said something in Hebrew. Then we each threw a handful of dirt into the grave, and Elza led me away while Namir and Dustin did the heavy work.

# 17

Roz had called a meeting of all the adults, newcomers and old residents, outside the dining hall in last light. There were over a hundred, mostly sitting on the ground or leaning against buildings. She began without preamble.

"We've all heard the same rumors. Some are exaggerated. There isn't a huge army gathering out there in the woods. But there is a large and growing number of people, not as many as we have here. They have weapons and ammunition and a dwindling amount of food.

"Some people who joined us today confirmed that they have leadership, a coalition of two biker gangs from San Francisco."

The "biker gangs" were social clubs with two hundred years of history. They began as warring clans who roamed the old highway system on compact armed motorcycles, gasoline-powered until that became an expensive anachronism. They evolved into respected service organizations whose public appearance reflected their land-pirate origins. Mostly men, mostly fat and bearded, wearing leather clothing and tattoos. The leader would have an expensive loud antique gasoline motorcycle; the others, quiet electric scooters. They organized charity drives and always showed up in formation for parades and big games.

A few of the gangs had gone back to their violent origins years before the power went off. Then they junked their useless vehicles and took bicycles.

They knew which towns were not well defended, and raided their stores. The concentration of guns and ammunition at Funny Farm had protected them from individual gangs—but that concentration was also irreplaceable wealth in what had become a desperate firearm culture. So both large gangs had gotten together to plan a joint raid.

People who had come into the stockade for protection had wildly varying estimates of the size of the biker coalition, from a hundred to a thousand.

A hundred would be a manageable annoyance. A thousand would conquer the farm and take everything.

Namir knew how to conduct interrogations; that was his job description in a dark period of his life. Funny Farm didn't have any of the advanced tools of the trade, but as Roz saw, he had full control of the basic ones: voice, manner, posture. A small room with one door and no windows.

She asked him to talk to each of the informers individually, alone. He didn't raise a hand against them, or even his voice, but he got as much of the truth as they could give.

"The two gangs in charge," Roz continued, "the Fangs and the Crips, have worked together before. They attacked compounds like ours—Bakersfield and Torrance—and left behind nothing but smoking ruins and corpses.

"The Fangs take female prisoners, for sex, but they don't live long. When it comes to fighting, I want all of us women to remember that. Be fierce. There are"—she cleared her throat—"there are better ways to die. There are worse things than dying.

"We're going to pull everyone inside the walls except for three scouts. They might be able to give us early warning; they might even infiltrate the enemy force and do some damage from inside. They don't have specific orders.

"The rest of us stay inside the walls and hope they hold. The Crips have some military explosives, though they may have used them up cracking into Bakersfield. They had real walls there; it used to be a prison.

"They'll probably attack sooner rather than later. They must be close to maximum force now, so have no reason to put it off."

"They'll wait until dark," said a gray-bearded man leaning against the wall behind her. "While it's light, they're sittin' ducks."

She nodded. "Before dark we want to have all the weapons and ammunition sorted out. I don't think they'll likely attack from the front or rear, at least not at first, because there's not much to hide behind.

"By Wham-O's count, we have a basic armament of seventeen assault rifles, using the same military ammo, with only about sixty cartridges apiece, so we have to be prudent there. Likewise, Carmen brought a belt-fed machine gun, but with how many rounds?"

"Only ninety-seven," I said. "Maybe thirty seconds' worth."

"We have three shotguns in different sizes, each with maybe a dozen shells. Namir has suggested that we not use them until the enemy is coming over the walls, or is inside."

"We may lose a wall," Namir said, "if they use explosives. So 'inside' becomes moot. Everybody tie a white cloth above your left biceps." He had a pillowcase full of strips torn from a sheet. "At least at first, we'll be able to tell friend from foe that way in the dark.

"I don't suppose we have a strategy beyond the obvious. Fire from shelter, and don't let them take shelter. Don't shoot each other.

"The four of us from the starship will take care of the southeast tower," he said, pointing. "Everybody else meet with Roz now in the dining hall. She has a chart with nighttime positions." She nodded and led them away.

I watched them going with a rising sense of hopeless fear, panic. I wanted to run, and there was no place to go.

Elza and Dustin, holding hands, exchanged a wordless communication with Namir, and went off together for a little privacy. "Aren't you ever afraid?" I said.

He gave me a troubled look and touched my arm, an electric tingle. "Always a little. We've gotten through worse things."

But always with Paul, I thought. "So what should I do with these things?" I had the machine gun, as long as a rifle but heavier, and the plastic ammo box that weighed about ten pounds, as well as an assault rifle and a pistol.

"I'll help you carry them up the tower. I guess Dustin should shoot the machine gun, unless you want to."

"Oh, sure. As long as I don't have to hit anything specific." Or at all.

The rest of us could crowd in there with him, with rifles and the night glasses. That was what he called the big binoculars, which showed more at night, even without electronics. "Do the three-on, one-off shifts." He smiled. "Two on, two off for now."

I followed him across the compound to the tower, where we relieved a girl who did look relieved. She couldn't have been fourteen, shorter than the old rifle she passed down.

There was a large wicker basket raised and lowered by a pulley, so you didn't have to negotiate the ladder carrying things. Namir scrambled up as soon as the girl came down, and I passed up all the armaments and ammunition, along with two canteens and some bread. I got halfway up the ladder and realized I'd better go pee first, so did.

The tower was cozy but not too crowded, about six feet square. The outside walls were reinforced with thick logs, virtually bullet-proof. A plank shelf, waist high, held all the ammunition, separated by type. Namir made sure I could locate them by touch.

We looked out over the wheat field and the approach road, with woods to our right. The foliage became thick a couple of dozen yards out.

"That's the way they'll come," I said.

"If they hit this site at all. If they attack at all."

"You wouldn't."

"No." I could just see his face in the fading light, his lips pursing. "You try to get inside the enemy's head. But there's a limit to 'what would I do in this situation?'—when you'd never be *in* this situation. The countryside is full of soft targets, where they could just walk in and wave some guns around and take what they want. So why attack a fortress?"

"Because it's there?"

"Some version of that. The challenge."

"Plunder," I said.

"What?"

"They are pirates; you called them that. They want plunder, treasure. Funny Farm has the equivalent of gold and pieces of eight. Ammunition and food."

"Alcohol and women," he said. "And all this low technology, if they've thought that far. Lights and machinery that work without power."

It had become too dark to see the shelf. I reached out and touched the rifle magazines, the box of pistol cartridges, the machine gun's ammo box, with the long belt protruding. A short belt, nineteen rounds, was already locked and loaded.

He could tell what I was doing. "How do you feel about reloading the machine gun in the dark?"

"Rather you do it."

"Okay." He stepped around me and picked up the weapon and its plastic box. Propped it next to him and peered out into the gathering dark. "If they're smart, they're sleeping now. Rest up and hit us a few hours after midnight. Meanwhile, send out decoys now and then to keep us nervous and burn up our ammo.

"They could do that for days," I said.

"And they might, if they were a well-organized army. I think they're itching for action and their leaders, if they have leaders, know they'll be losing people every day. They'll hit tonight. The only question is how long will they wait?"

As if in answer, one shot on the other side. I faintly heard a male voice, maybe Wham-O, saying, "Don't!" There was no return fire.

"Flash suppressor," Namir said, and I checked mine, though I remembered sliding it into place.

"Don't start without us," Elza said from the ladder. She crawled up onto the floor, and Dustin handed up two rifles and followed her.

"What do you think?" he said, panting.

Another shot on the other side. "I think 'lock and load.'" Sound of greased metal, rifles being cocked. I heard Namir move the machine gun around, rattle and sweep of its ammunition belt. "This machine gun, we'll wait for clear targets. Every fourth round's a tracer." We knew that, of course. It would draw attention.

"Dustin, you do bursts of three. The rest of us go single-shot for the time being?" His voice was calm, except for an edge that wasn't fear. He was looking forward to it, in his way.

He once told me that up to a certain point, every battle you survive makes the next one easier. But everyone had a limit. Once you've cracked, you are like a pot that has cracked. Not very useful.

Maybe some of us were different. Maybe we started out cracked.

Another shot, and then another. My mouth and throat went dry, and I concentrated on keeping my nether parts the same.

I heard Elza unscrew a bottle and smelled sweet wine. "Here, Carmen." It helped my throat a little, but my stomach was a knot.

Just get on with it. Please just do it. I suddenly realized that the people in the woods must feel the same way. You may not want it to happen, but even more, you don't want to wait any longer.

"Places," Namir said. "Carmen, come up to my left." For a panicked moment, I couldn't remember which was which. "Dustin, Elza, magazines on the shelf at waist height. Five or six?"

They moved into place, and I could hear them counting with their hands. They murmured assent, and the wind brought the smell of powder.

There was a loud deep pound, a shotgun, and someone screamed in pain, "My hand! My *hand*!"

Then the gunfire started crackling, that dreadful popcorn sound. "Hold fire," Namir said conversationally. "Let them waste it."

There was a loud thump, and then three more, as bullets struck our walls. They were thick split logs on the sides that faced out. "Hope they don't have anything bigger," Dustin said. Thanks.

"Give me the pistol, Carmen," Namir said. "Guy right down on the edge." I should've thought to close my eyes. Under our roof it was darker than night. When the pistol went off, it was a bright blue flash, and I was blind except for the strobe image of Namir aiming down.

"Think I got him. Can you see, Carmen?"

"Not yet."

"I can," Dustin said, and I heard him shuffle over to Namir's window.

"By the main door, the side facing us."

"Yeah, I see. Not moving." Someone fired a long burst in our direction; I felt Dustin duck as it stuttered on the walls. One round came through the slot and banged into the metal roof. "Shit," he whispered. His head could've been there.

Or mine. The wine surged up and I swallowed it back, then drank half a canteen of water on top of it. Just don't puke. Do, my body answered. I wasn't going to stick my head out the window, but I made it to the door, and decorated the ladder.

"Thanks for waiting," Dustin said. Elza handed me a towel that smelled of sweat, but I managed not to barf again. Sat back and picked up the heavy rifle and held the cold metal to my cheek for a moment, smell of gun oil and powder.

"I'll be okay," I said to no one, and no one believed me.

There was a loud explosion to the left and a sudden yellow glare. "Fire bomb, damn!" Namir said.

I scooted over on my butt and crouched up far enough to see the flames. The double door in the front was covered with some burning liquid. Someone downstairs yelled "Fire!" and a gong clanged three times.

They had a leg-powered pump, a converted bicycle, that brought water from the pond to the kitchen. I wondered whether its hose would reach that far.

"Targets," Namir said quietly, and fired three spaced shots. Then he ducked down. The shotgun boomed, and a few pellets rattled against the roof.

"Almost out of range," Dustin said.

"Like to get him anyhow." Namir said. He put his cap on the muzzle of the rifle and lifted it up to draw fire, but the enemy weren't fooled, or couldn't see. Or were being frugal with ammunition.

"Namir," came a hoarse shout from below. He stepped over to the ladder and nodded down at the man.

"We got to open the door to get the hose to it. Need you to keep their heads down."

"We'll try. In ten seconds?"

"Ten." I heard steps running away and started counting.

At what I counted to be eight seconds, Namir's machine gun started chattering. One long burst, then two short ones, and he ducked back behind the logs. I heard him slap open the top of the receiver and install the last belt.

He left the machine gun on the floor and stood up with a rifle. His face was plain in the light from the burning door. He stared for a second, then aimed and squeezed off one round. He ducked.

"Let's not draw too much attention now. Take single shots, one person at a time."

I stood up and pointed the rifle down at the trees. A lot of shooting but no obvious target. I pulled the trigger at nothing and crouched back down.

The shot had made me deaf in one ear, but I think Namir said, "Good." Well, I didn't shoot any of us.

"This place needs a periscope," Elza said, standing up and aiming. She fired, maybe at random, and ducked back down. "Put it on the list."

There was a new kind of explosion, a sound like whish-*bang*! "Rocket," Namir said. Then a sudden bright blue flickering light.

Namir squinted into it. "Jesus! Everyone up and shoot!" He started firing fast single shots.

I jumped up next to him and aimed down. In the light of a guttering magnesium flare, I could see that they'd blown the double doors down and were charging en masse down the road and across the corn stubble. Dozens of people, maybe a hundred, most of them not shooting, intent on their charge.

A few people in front stopped long enough to kneel and fire over the smoldering door, into the stockade.

One of them was Card. Still wearing the dirty white tourist suit.

I aimed at him but couldn't pull the trigger. Instead, I fired into the crowd behind him, and two men dropped. Or women or children. Fired twice more, trying to aim, and missed. When I looked for Card again, he was gone.

"That was Card!" I said. I don't know whether anyone responded. There was an explosion under our feet, and suddenly flames everywhere in front.

Namir yelled something and pushed me roughly toward the ladder. I got halfway down and slipped.

Banged to my knee on the ladder and hurt both ankle and shoulder, somehow, when I hit the ground.

The rifle clattered down a few feet away. I went over to it and had the presence of mind to make sure it hadn't landed nose first, then aimed it at the open door, where a little fire still flickered.

"Over here!" Namir was crouched behind one of the pilings that supported the lookout we'd just deserted. The side facing out was starting to burn.

Elza was next to him, helping set up the machine gun. Dustin hit the ground heavily between us and rolled toward me. He shook his head, dazed.

Namir called out again, and Dustin looked over dumbly and collapsed. I crawled by him, dragging my rifle.

"Anyone without an armband," he said. Two or three people were already shooting over the fallen door. Two attackers almost got inside; sprawled dead or dying on the threshold.

"What, are they suicidal?" I said, aiming at the space.

"Desperate." Another one appeared and was shot down, then three more. Namir was holding his fire.

Then someone hurled a fire bomb, gasoline or something, halfway to the center of the compound—and dozens boiled through the door, shooting and screaming.

✳

Namir fired a burst, then a sustained chatter. They kept coming, though, crawling over the fallen, trying to run left and right.

Shooting back. Even over the machine-gun racket, I could hear bullets hissing by.

I mimicked Namir and lay prone, presenting as small a target as possible.

This had happened often enough that the physical sensation was almost familiar. Time crawled. My face and hands were greasy with cold sweat. All tight inside. Wiping away tears and snot.

"Shoot, goddamn it!" Dustin shouted. I'd fired one burst and still held the trigger down in a spastic clench. I pulled it again and again, firing in the direction of the crowd pushing through the door.

When I was young, I wondered about the expression "shooting fish in a barrel"—the image was so silly. Besides, you could just shoot a hole in the barrel and let the water drain out. That's what this was, though. Or lemmings, another animal metaphor that had nothing to do with reality. Rushing through the door as if it were the edge of a cliff.

It couldn't have taken long. Finally, two of them used the pile of bodies as a kind of shield, firing machine guns blindly toward us from behind their dead and dying comrades. The bullets went well over my head as I hugged the ground between Namir and Dustin. In less than a minute, someone shot the two from a rooftop, and all was quiet.

Relatively quiet. Someone was crying, and another groaned over and over. Namir ran to the pile of bodies and tossed away the rifles the two had been shooting. He studied the pile, I guess for signs of life. Then he peered out from behind the door for a few seconds and pulled his head back in.

*Don't do that,* I almost yelled. *Don't push your luck.* How many had held back from the charge?

A minute went by, then several, without a shot. Some people came out of the main cabin with candles and first-aid kits and began circulating.

One of them, a woman I hadn't met, came over to us.

"Any wounded?"

My ankle hurt like hell, but it wasn't broken. I remembered what that felt like, from the night I fell into a lava tube and was discovered by the Martians. When I was a frightened girl, studying to be a terrified woman.

"Check Dustin over there. I think he was knocked out." I watched her in the candlelight. She felt for a pulse in his neck and wrist.

"He's alive," she said, and he reached up weakly and touched her face.

"There it is again," Namir said. He was looking up.

The bright blue light, unblinking, moving slowly overhead. Some idiot fired a machine gun at it, tracers slowing and falling away. It shrank to a dim point and disappeared.

"Brilliant," he said. "Let's see whether they shoot back."

They didn't, and the incident was forgotten in the confused aftermath of the attack. Eight people had serious wounds. They rigged a fly for shelter on the side of the infirmary and put the wounded on makeshift pallets there, along with an operating table; there wasn't enough light inside for surgery.

They were long out of glue, and had to stitch people up. Running out of everything else. Two of the enemy bled to death because the farm was rationing its supply of surrogate.

It would run out sooner or later, of course, along with everything else medical. Those medical books from the 1800s that we brought from Lanny's would eventually save a lot of lives. But first a few people, a few million, would have to die from lack of everyday miracles, like nanotech and blood surrogate.

They did have a stretchy ankle bandage to keep me upright and working. I slept for a couple of fitful hours and then was up at dawn to work a grave-digging shift. There were individual graves for the dead farmers, but what I and five others were working on was a mass shallow grave for the eighteen enemy dead. It was a pyre as much as a grave, actually. Hip deep, twelve feet by six. We filled it with dry wood and kindling and stacked pine logs on that. And then the bodies.

I was glad to be excused from that part of it. There were plenty of enthusiastic volunteers.

A vocal minority wanted them stripped. Manufactured clothing would be rare soon. Okay, Roz said—you can take it, but you have to wear it yourself. No one did.

It was a horrible sight. Faces blackening and melting in the flames, restless dead limbs moving, insides boiling away and bursting, the fire bright and greasy with rendered human fat. Finally, it was only skeletons and separated bones momentarily glimpsed inside the roaring flames.

Part of me watched the process with numb detachment. I didn't even notice when Namir left my side and then came back with a cup of wine, which he offered to me.

"No," I said. "I'm still queasy."

"Yes," he said, and stared at the fire as he drank. He smiled, and I wondered what he was thinking. Maybe I didn't want to know.

"Got some more for you," Roz said, approaching with Jerry pulling the cart. Seven or eight bodies, all apparently men. "Let's check all the pockets for ammo before they go into the fire."

I reached for the top body and jumped back. It was Card.

"Sorry," Roz said, recognizing him. "I'll do it."

His face was unaffected, calm. But the top of his head had been blown out of round by a bullet that hit him in the temple. On the other side, an exit wound the size of my fist.

"He didn't feel anything," I said.

"A pity." She pulled him off the cart by his feet and dragged him partway to the fire. She turned out his pockets, found something, and held it out to me. "Yours if you want it."

It was a keychain with two old-fashioned metal keys as well as modern stubs. It was attached to a little carving that I immediately recognized: a small sea tortoise carved from a tagera nut in the Galápagos—my parents had bought them as souvenirs for us before we got on the Space Elevator on the way to Mars.

Mine was still on Mars, in a box of personal effects I'd left behind.

"Thanks," I said, and stared at it as she and two other women carried his body away. I turned my back toward them so as not to watch him consigned to the flames. There was no love between us, but a lot of history.

My last blood connection to the Earth. Parents long gone and both my children Martians. "Back in a minute," I said to no one in particular, and headed for the latrine. It wasn't the most pleasant place to sit and think, but if I spent enough time there, the next time I looked into the fire, I wouldn't recognize anybody. And the heat from the flames suddenly felt monstrous.

# 18

By the next morning, the fire had burned all the way down, and there was nothing recognizably human on the surface of the ashes. Those of us who had dug the pits were given a morning of rest while different work crews filled them.

I volunteered to take some tea and cookies out to them, mid-morning, which was good fortune for me, if not for them. I dropped the tray. But I got to see the Martians land.

A huge floating disc, maybe half the size of the entire compound, floated swiftly down out of the sky and stopped, hovering a couple of feet off the ground. There was no sound except for the crash of my teapot and cups.

"Please do not shoot," the disc said with an amplified American accent. "We're unarmed; we mean no harm. Hello, Carmen."

"Hello," I said. "I know you?"

"No. But there are people aboard you do know." There was a dome-shaped protrusion in the center of the disc. A wedge of door opened, facing us.

A Martian stepped out and rippled toward the edge of the disc, all of its arms out in greeting.

"Snowbird?"

"It's good to see you, Carmen. Paul is not with you."

"He died . . . he died a couple of days ago."

"I am sorry we missed him. We could use another pilot. It's a long way back home."

"Siberia?"

"Back to Mars. Home."

"It came from Russia to pick me up? Us?"

"They picked *me* up in Russia, Carmen. They came from Mars, of course."

"We are trying to locate every surviving Martian on Earth," the amplified voice said. "You and Paul appear to be the last."

Namir had come up beside me. "Leaving . . . for good?" he said.

"We don't know," the voice said. "This is all native Martian technology, which is to say, it's from the Others. It might last forever, it might crash today. All we know for sure is that we can't touch the surface of the Earth. If we do that, the power dies."

"We had to jump on board," Snowbird said, "from a snow-covered roof."

"I'm afraid there's not much time," the voice said. "In the absence of Paul, you could bring another. But you have to decide now."

I turned to Namir. His eyes were wide. Elza stepped up next to him, without touching, her face a mask. "Go with her," she said softly. "You have to."

Dustin limped up and put his hand on her shoulder. "For both of us," he said. "For all of us. Go."

Namir embraced them both, and said something I couldn't hear.

Then he turned his back on everything and held out his hand to me.

His hand was large and strong. The skin was rough. "Shall we?"

We took two steps together and leaped into space.

# Epilogue

It's been a long time since dying was simple. When I returned to Mars, almost forty ares ago, two of the first people I met were my dead brother.

Before the Others pulled the plug on the Earth, back in 2138, there had been a constant data exchange between the two planets for most of a century. Absolutely total backup, which included the cybernetic copies of Card's two reserve bodies, although they were physically destroyed along with Los Angeles.

Of course there are billions of such "people," sitting around as passive records, whose physical bodies are long gone. Some of them even had citizenship, back on Earth, if they'd filed the right incorporation papers before they died. Card had. I guess he could still vote in California if anyone was running for office.

I talk to one or the other every now and then, but it's creepy. The calendar peeps me when it would be their birthday on Earth. His birthday.

They've never asked me about the day that he died.

If only my parents had lived long enough to be duplicated; I'd love to talk to either of them. They might not have done it anyhow. I haven't. It takes weeks of immersion, and a desire to outlive your body.

I may do it yet. Both universities are after me, so all this valuable history should not be lost.

But maybe it should be lost. It's not as if they don't make new history to take its place.

When my dear Namir died, after we'd been together almost thirty ares, he declined to leave a copy. He quoted Wordsworth to me: "The old order changeth, making place for new / And God fulfils himself in many ways."

He didn't believe in gods any more than I do. But it's a convenient shorthand.

Twice in these forty ares we have seen signs of life, communications, from Earth. There's a powerful telescope at the observatory that's dedicated to that task, at least one person watching the Earth whenever it's up.

During the second-most-recent opposition, a tiny cross burned in Siberia, the place where Martians last lived on Earth. Each arm of the cross was forty miles long, so it was quite an engineering feat with primitive tools. Twenty ares before, a fiery cross—or X— appeared in the desert of White Sands, New Mexico, and was visible as a black mark on Earth's crescent for months.

They are still there. Still looking up.

Sometimes before dawn or just after sunset, I go up into the old dome and watch the blue spark of Earth rising or setting.

I did that this morning, for no special reason on the Martian calendar, but mine peeped and reminded me that on Earth I would be ninety years old today. Or my bones would be.

So I carried these old bones up and sat there alone, watching the Earth fade as the sky went from indigo to pale orange. Remembering the morning more than seventy years ago, waiting for a cab in the Florida dark. My father pointing out the bright unblinking red dot that we were about to visit. Saying we'd be back home in about five years.

But home was where we were going.